DIARY OF AN unwilling SUPERHERO

**Written & Illustrated
by
Rosemary Sixbey**

DEDICATION

To all the unwilling heroes out there
who've had to battle unexpected villains.

TRIGGER WARNING

Unexpected and horrible things are depicted in this book.
That's how life happens sometimes.

April 9th

My new job blew up on me today.

This was the temp job at Globotek. And I admit, it was hardly an exciting gig. Coffee, mail, and front desk smiles. The usual white-collar option for an un-colleged gal like myself. But it was a paycheck, and WorldPro Temp Agency had said the job might turn permanent, if things went well.

I arrived bright and early for my first day on the job. My hair was blond, coifed, and cute. I was wearing my short-skirted, bright pink business suit – the one my roommate Neal says makes me look like a bimbo, but what does he know. Besides, looking like a bimbo isn't always a bad thing when you're bucking for a secretary job to a wealthy businessman.

The building was impressive. It really was. The reception area was grand and spacious with thirty-foot windows and real oak furniture. In the middle of the room was a gigantic, circular reception desk. Above it on the far wall was a larger-than-life portrait of a portly businessman wearing a monocle. The air smelled of cleaning solutions from the janitor's work the previous night. No doubt about it. This was the kind of place that offered 401Ks.

Oh yeah. I wanted this job.

My supervisor was a nerd named Edwin Peabody. And believe me when I say nerd. He was a science nerd in its purest form. White coat, thick-rimmed glasses that might have looked sexy on a different man, but somehow made him look awkward and pathetic. His clothing was too big. But he got a big, endearing grin on his face when he talked about the work of the lab. I liked him. I could have him wrapped

around my finger by the end of the day.

Edwin started the obligatory office tour, which in this case meant one meaningless white hallway after another, filled with identical closed doors. Edwin insisted that each one of them led to a lab or office where exciting, top-secret work was being done.

"Globotek's founder, Dr. Oswald Jaliswack, is a man of great vision, responsible for many of the great leaps in the radiological sciences," Edwin was saying proudly. "I'm sure you noticed his portrait in the reception hall. As you are already aware, this branch of Globotek is doing some truly ground-breaking exploration into the effects of gamma radiation on genetics in micro-animals...." He guided me through maze-like hallways and droned on about the research of the lab and how it was going to save the world or something for the better part of an hour. I smiled and said "Impressive!" at all the right moments and dutifully followed behind him. But I paid absolutely no attention to what he was saying.

Just when my head was about to explode with boredom, Edwin was thankfully interrupted by a call to his cell phone. "Oh dear," he said into the phone. "Oh dear, oh dear... you need me right now? Right absolutely right now? Okay. I'll send our new girl on ahead and come find you."

Edwin furrowed his brow, shifting his large glasses crookedly on his face. "I'm being called away, Annie," he told me. "You go down the rest of this hallway into Laboratory 735. They'll direct you from there, and we can get started. I... I really am so very glad that you have joined us here." He motioned vaguely down the corridor in front of us, turned back in the direction we'd come from, and dashed off.

I was left alone in the silent walls. I walked down the hallway, looking for Laboratory 735. Strangely, the rooms were not in number order. First, I passed Office 965. Next, I passed Laboratory 12. After that were a couple of bathrooms and a storage closet. But, eventually, I found Laboratory 735. I hesitated, but, having no idea how to get back to the reception desk without Edwin and wanting to make a proper impression, I opened the door.

It opened onto a narrow hallway with mirrored walls. There was something eerie about them. I had an instinctive feeling that I was being watched. I guarantee you those walls were two-way mirrors. I wondered who was on the other side.

"Hello?" I called out. There was no one there. "Hello!" I tried again. "It's Annie! Edwin sent me to you guys."

After about fifty feet, the mirrored hallway opened into a small circular room. Both the floor and ceiling were covered with dozens of circular lights. This place was getting creepy. But it was the first paying job I'd had in weeks, and my roommates were antsy for my share of the rent. I stepped into the room.

Within a second, a set of elevator-style doors snapped shut behind me. The lights in the ceiling and floor popped on. The gleaming light hurt my eyes. It was brighter than a tanning bed in there! I turned around, looking for another door, but I was trapped. "Hey!" I called out. I started banging on the door. "Hey! Hey! I'm in here!"

The lights glowed even brighter, and a whirring sound started. The noise grew louder and louder. An awful green smoke started to fill the room. Breathing it in made me cough and sputter. I dropped to the ground, but the smoke was coming up from vents in the floor. "Hey! Help me!" I cried out again, but I couldn't even hear my own voice over the whirring. My vision started growing fuzzy. I looked at my hands and saw multiple copies of them floating back and forth. I turned my head, and glowing tracers slinked out behind every object in my field of vision. I gasped for clean air that wasn't there. I lay on the ground and banged my fist feebly against the mirrored wall in soft, increasingly ineffective taps.

Then, suddenly, a thunderous boom cracked through the noise. The whirring stopped, the lights shut off, and the building shook violently. I was thrown to the far side of the room and plunged into darkness. My body smacked against the wall. I fell into a heap on the floor.

More thunderous explosions and crashing followed. The floor jolted back and forth. I was unable to move, but I opened my eyes. Sparks were leaping up from the lights in the floor. Flames were exploding into the air. A fire burst out right next to me. Then another and another, until everything around me was a blazing inferno.

I was so far gone that, as I lost consciousness, I swear I didn't even feel the heat.

When I awoke, I was in a pile of wreckage. In every direction, burnt and smoldering debris sent up smoke and foul stenches. *Dammit*, I thought to myself. The whole building had come down around me. One of my shoes had come off. Given how far the wreckage stretched, it looked like the parking lot was gone too. My purse, my wallet, my keys, my car... all blown to smithereens. Not to mention my new job and its 401K. I sorted through the steaming debris and found my other shoe. The heel had broken off. I shrugged, broke the heel off my good shoe, put them both back on, and awkwardly walked home.

Four miles later, sore and tired, but thankful that my

lazy roommate had forgotten to lock the back door again, I crawled into my bedroom, changed into pajamas, and fell fast asleep.

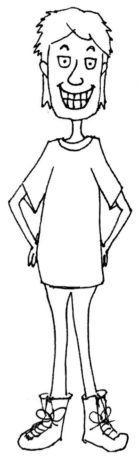

April 10th

When I stumbled downstairs to the kitchen the next morning, my roommates freaked out.

"Annie!" Neal screamed. "You're here! You're alive!"

Blossom rushed over and hugged me with such ferocity that she nearly knocked me off my feet.

"What's wrong with you two?" I grumbled, annoyed. The coffee pot looked suspiciously empty. I pulled out a new filter and started dumping coffee grounds into it.

"Globotek..." Neal said. "It's all over the news. The whole place exploded!"

"Oh that," I replied. "Yeah, it blew up alright. Came down all around me. It would have been a super good gig, too. It's too bad." I stared at the coffee grounds vacantly for a second. "Do you guys know how many scoops I put in here? I lost count."

Blossom grabbed me by the shoulders and stared me in the face. "Annie, how did you survive? They said everyone in the building was killed."

"We thought you were dead!" Neal exclaimed.

"I'm not dead." I threw a couple more scoops into the pot and turned it on. "It was totally crazy. The whole room was burning. Flames everywhere. And explosions, too. And there was this weird green smoke. I passed out and came home after I came to. I think my car blew up."

Neal and Blossom started getting these real strange looks on their faces. The coffee pot gurgled happily.

"What?" I finally said.

"Annie, did you say there were flames all around you?" Neal asked me.

"Yup," I told him. "The whole room I was in was an inferno."

"But..." Neal said. "You're not burned. Your hair isn't even singed."

I looked down at my arms and hands. My skin was smooth and clear. I reached up to my hair. It felt normal, just like they said. I turned and ran upstairs to my room. Neal and Blossom followed.

There, on the floor of my bedroom, lay the pink business suit I'd worn the day before. The fabric was blackened with smoke and soot. Holes had burnt through it. The zippers had liquefied and fused into misshapen masses of metal. The buttons had melted into plastic blobs on the fabric. The entire right sleeve was gone. All that was left was a singed armhole. You could barely tell it had once been a suit. I looked back at my skin – completely untouched by any hint of flame or burn.

I looked down at the suit, then up at my roommates. I suddenly felt wide awake.

"Hunh," I said.

Blossom and Neal spent the rest of the morning on the web, learning all they could about Globotek and the explosion. I sent an email off to WorldPro Temp Agency, asking for another assignment. Then I camped out at the breakfast table with my wrist hovering over a lit candle. The flames licked around both sides of my wrist. It was fun to watch. I bobbed my wrist up and down in the flame. I ran the flame up and down my arm. I tried my other arm. It was fascinating. I couldn't feel the heat. The flame didn't bother me in the slightest. Curious, I grabbed a paring knife from the kitchen and nicked the tip of my finger with it.

"Ouch!" I screamed, and I quickly got a bandage to mop up the blood. "Hey guys, it looks like I'm only invincible to flames, not to knives!" I called to my roommates helpfully.

"Did you just intentionally cut yourself? You idiot!" Blossom called back.

"Uh... no...." I lied.

Neal came in from the other room with a handful of articles pulled up on his laptop. I blew out my candle, and Blossom and I gathered round. "Globotek is an international multi-corporation that was founded twenty years ago by one Dr. Oswald Jaliswack," Neal began. "Previously unknown, he skyrocketed to power with a collection of amazing new advancements in the fields of genetic manipulation, medicine, and laser-based weaponry. Globotek has its hands in a little bit of everything, but most of it seems to be mining, weapons and genetics. The lab that blew up focused primarily on genetic manipulation."

I nodded. "Edwin said something about that. Micro-animals or something."

"I think you wandered into an experiment. Do you know what was going on in the room you were in?"

"No, I never even saw anyone in there. All I know is that it was Laboratory 735."

"Laboratory 735," Neal tapped out a few more inquiries on his laptop. "We need to find out what they were doing in that lab." He gave a suggestive look up at Blossom.

She shook her head. "Oh no," she said. "Absolutely not, no way. Uh-unh. Nope. Never."

"What?" I asked.

"If we want to find out more about what's going on," Neal said to Blossom, "we need your Uncle Archie. We need his secret lair."

"Secret lair?" I asked.

Blossom cringed. "That guy is creepy and a half. And, yes, he has a secret lair." She shuddered. "Okay. I'll text him that we're coming over. But we're not staying for cakes and tea. This is an information-only expedition."

Blossom's uncle lived an hour away in the rolling hills of the countryside. We piled out of Neal's car, and I got my first taste of what we were in for. The place was a manor—I'd never seen a house that large before, outside of a magazine or a British television show. A foreboding wrought-iron gate ringed the perimeter of the property, which went on as far as the eye could see. The house itself was four stories tall and countless windows wide. The driveway was a large swooping circle with a fountain in the middle. The fountain statue was of a great warrior atop a three-headed dragon. The dragon's wings arched out, and the fountain's water shot out of the dragon's three mouths like giant roaring flames. The walls of the manor were thick grey stone. Gargoyles perched high above on the roof and peered down inquisitively from second-story balconies.

"Who *is* this guy?" I gawked as I took it all in. "It's like Count Dracula's manor."

"More than you know, darling," mumbled Blossom, as she pushed past me and up to the front doors, which must have stood twelve feet tall. More mini-gargoyles peered out from around the corners of the door. Their eyes glowed red and gold. Blossom lifted the large brass knocker and gave it a loud rap.

The man who opened the door belonged in the manor. He was tall and lean with a long, pointy face. Spiky grey hair sprouted from his head in all directions. He wore spotless white gloves and a green velvet suit that was immaculately cleaned and pressed.

"Blossom!" he cried out. "My delicate summer flower!" He thrust out his arms for an embrace. She shouldered past him.

"Uncle Archie," she said flatly. "We'll be leaving soon."

He next turned to me, and his face glowed. His eyes were the brightest blue I'd ever seen on a grown man. "And you must be the remarkable Miss Annie Glenn. I cannot describe my excitement at meeting you. My name is Lord Archibald Feathering."

He grasped his hand in mine, stepped back into a bow, and planted a delicate kiss on my fingers. I couldn't help but blush. This guy was unreal!

He turned my hand over in his palm. "Remarkable, my dear, remarkable. Indeed, no evidence of the fire! And Globotek, you say? Remarkable, indeed."

"She's dating someone," Blossom interjected.

"That's not true," I brushed her off.

Lord Feathering took my hand and looked straight into my eyes. "Come, come, come, my dear. You have earned your way to my underground laboratory. We shall run some tests and find out just what has befallen you."

Lord Feathering led me down the hall, which was decorated with red scarlet tapestries, medieval suits of armor, and countless pieces of weaponry. Blossom and Neal followed behind. Halfway down the hall, Lord Feathering turned to me and winked.

"You'll like this part," he said slyly. He took hold of one of the wall sconces and rotated it to the left, then right, then left. A combination lock. You could hear the pop as the locking mechanisms snapped into place. A hidden door swung open in the wall. I laughed out loud in surprise. Lord Feathering beamed and led us down a twisting stone staircase, two or three levels below the ground.

The stairwell opened up into an underground cavern. On one side was stacked rows upon rows of computer servers, neatly connected with countless cords. A half-circle desk of keyboards and a wall of monitors stood nearby.

"I'm getting on your network," Neal said to Lord Feathering. He hopped over to the computers and cracked his knuckles excitedly. The screens sprang to life, and he began his work. Lord Feathering appeared to be aware of Neal's actions but was not interested enough to respond.

The rest of the massive room was piled high with all manner of scientific equipment and gadgets. Some of the devices I recognized — test tubes, Bunsen burners, high-powered microscopes, a centrifuge. But some of the others I could not even imagine what their purposes might be. Lord Feathering guided me through the maze of devices, still holding my hand with the delicacy of a gentleman.

"My darling," he said to me. "I am afraid I will have to trouble you for a bit of your blood."

I smiled. Count Dracula indeed.

"And your DNA," he added.

He pulled out a sterile kit of needles. I couldn't help but wonder why he had them in stock. With quick and expert fingers, he cleaned my arm, popped a needle into it, and drew out a small vial of blood.

"I'm impressed," I told him. "The nurses always have to give a few pokes before they hit the vein."

He snarled at the word *nurses*. "Amateurs," he hissed, and he pulled out a cotton swab. "And, if you would be so kind as to scrape this along the inside of your mouth."

I gave him the DNA sample.

"And now, my dear, I must ask you to leave me be," he said kindly. "I would offer you cakes and tea while you wait, but I fear some of my tests will take hours to complete. I shall contact you tomorrow morning with my findings."

"Let's go!" Blossom said cheerfully, having appeared from out of nowhere. She grabbed me by the arm and pulled me off toward the secret staircase.

"I'm staying," Neal called to us. "I'll be able to find out everything we need about Globotek from here."

"Cheerio!" Blossom called back to him. She kept a vice-like grip on my upper arm and pulled me up the stairs. Within twenty seconds, we were burning rubber in Neal's car as she tore out of the driveway and onto the main road.

"I hate that place," Blossom explained with a smile.

April 11th

My phone beeped that a new email message was arriving. "Woohoo!" I cried out at the breakfast table. WorldPro Temp Agency had a new gig for me. Another receptionist position starting that very morning. I threw on my second-best receptionist outfit – a short-skirted baby blue business suit. Hair curl enhancer, an extra bit of makeup. I scribbled a note to Blossom and Neal and hopped on the bus.

Talon Falls Industrial was in a dreary business park just outside of town. A grey-haired woman at the front desk greeted me. "Are you Abby, the temp?" she asked me.

"Annie, yes, it's good to –" I began.

"Oh, thank heavens, they were convinced you wouldn't show." She spun around and disappeared through a black security door.

Left alone, I looked around awkwardly and took a seat on the green vinyl waiting chairs. My phone beeped at me that a call was coming in. It was Neal.

"Hi there!" I answered the phone. A burst of static.

"I'm not getting a signal in here, Neal," I said. "I'll call you later."

I hung up. Instantly it began ringing again. I replied with a text that I was at my new job and would call him later.

Neal texted me back. Just as I was about to check it, the black security door opened. The grey-haired woman appeared in the doorway and gestured me inside. "They're ready for you now," she said, a polite smile pasted on her face. I followed her.

She led me down a bland hallway and into a strange room. It was set up like a normal business office, except for one wall, on which hung a variety of medical tools and gadgets. There was a second door, opposite me. On either side of it stood two large men in navy blue suits. Neither of them spoke. The woman gestured for me to have a seat, which I did. She spun about and left the room, the door clicking shut behind her.

This temp job was beginning to seem strange. My phone beeped that another text was coming through. I smiled at the two men, who offered no response, and I pulled out my cell phone. I had five new messages from Neal, all the same.

"DO NOT GO TO TEMP JOB. WORLDPRO TEMP AGENCY IS OWNED BY GLOBOTEK. ALL A

SET UP. USING YOU FOR AN EXPERIMENT. THEY CANNOT BE TRUSTED."

I gulped, and before I could think, the door between the two men opened and in walked the nerd from Globotek, Edwin Peabody. I sure was surprised to see him! I'd figured he'd gotten blown up along with everything else. But what was he doing here? Neal must be right. I glanced nervously toward the door.

"Annie!" he greeted me with a warm smile. "It is such a relief to see you. I apologize for the subterfuge in bringing you here on another temp job. We didn't know how else to get ahold of you. We are so relieved to see that you survived the accident."

"Accident!" I cried out. "The entire building blew up!"

"It was a *big* accident, wasn't it?" Edwin agreed, pushing his glasses up as he spoke. "And one that attracted rather more attention than desired at this stage of our research. We shall have to move quickly if we are to complete the rest of our work in time. Unfortunately, so much was destroyed in the explosion. Such a setback, such a setback...." He shook his head and threw up his hands. "But it is a good sign that you survived. Now, let's start by getting a quick sample of your blood."

He pulled out a syringe from the wall of medical supplies and took my arm. He looked at me apologetically. "Hold your arm still, please. I'm afraid it's been a while since I've drawn blood. I was in charge of the labs at

Globotek. I had my staff to do all the tech work. I hope you can appreciate, Annie, how grateful we are all that you survived. Your survival means we might just have a chance. It's the breakthrough we've been working toward."

Holding my arm awkwardly, he jabbed me with the needle. A shooting pain went through my arm. "OW!" I screamed and jerked my body back. "Actually, Edwin," I told him, "I think I'd better be going. I'll have to get back to you later with the blood sample."

I stepped back, turned and walked rather quickly over to the exit door. I yanked at the handle and found that I was locked in.

"Oh dear, oh dear," said a flustered Edwin. He shook his head disagreeably. "No, this won't do. This won't do at all. Annie, you must help us. This is your job from here on out."

"I didn't agree to be experimented on!" I snapped back.

He looked genuinely confused. "But you did!" he said simply. "WorldPro had you sign all the paperwork. And you were so excited about the project when I was giving you the tour... We're going to do such good work together! Why are you changing your mind?" The nerd looked so sad and dejected that I almost felt sorry for him.

I stood there in the office, not knowing what to do. I flashed back to the pages of paperwork that WorldPro Temp had had me sign. I had read none of it, of course. And then I remembered how Edwin had talked excitedly for almost an hour on our tour, and how I hadn't listened to any of it.

What had I gotten myself into?

"I'm sorry, Edwin," I told him. "I truly am. But there's been a misunderstanding. I thought I was signing up to be a receptionist, not a lab rat."

"A lab rat!" he exclaimed disgustedly. "Is that what you call the woman who's going to save our world?"

I shook my head. "Edwin, you have to unlock this door. I am no longer here willingly. You have to let me go now."

He seemed dumbfounded. Then resigned. "I see I have no choice," he said. I breathed a sigh of relief. Then Edwin glanced at the two large men and gave them a quick nod. They walked across the room and stood directly on my left and right. That's when it dawned on me. These guys weren't businessmen. They were thugs, and they were towering over me.

As women go, I'm neither large nor strong. I stand 5'5" on a good day, and my heals push me up only a little bit higher. I've got nice boobs and a curve to my hips, but basically, I'm a twig. A twig that could be snapped in half by either of these men in a second. I flashed back to the karate classes I took in high school. I'd gotten as far as my green belt and wasn't bad at sparring and take-downs. But that was almost ten years ago, and I'd been sparring against boys who hadn't hit puberty yet. I desperately wished for a moment that I was Blossom. That woman is large and powerful. She's got a hundred pounds on me easily. Her biceps are like locomotives.

But I'm not Blossom. And I'm not a black belt. I'm a twig in a mini-skirted baby blue business suit. And I did what any good blond in high heels would do in a horror movie.

I panicked and screamed like a girl.

"Help! Let me out! Let me out!" I turned and banged on the door.

The two men grabbed me, one by each arm. I kicked and squirmed and screamed as they lifted me up and carried me back over to Edwin. One held me in a bear hug. The other grabbed my arm and held it plastered against the table for Edwin and his needle. I struggled with all my force. I'd never felt so powerless. I was completely unable to free myself. My feet weren't even touching the ground. I kicked and kicked and then one of the men slapped me hard across the face. "Quit squirming," he boomed at me.

Edwin was most put out. "Don't you hurt her," he scolded the thug, shaking a skinny finger at him. "This is the woman who is going to save our world. She is to be treated with the utmost respect!"

He laid a hand on my arm and jabbed the syringe into it. Then slowly, carefully, he pulled out a vial of blood. I tried to squirm, but every time I moved with the needle in my arm it only caused more pain.

Then suddenly there was pandemonium. Out of nowhere, a giant black armored car came crashing through the office wall. Broken glass, concrete, and medical supplies went flying everywhere. The thugs were so surprised that they loosened their grips on me. I broke away from them.

The side door of the car swung open. Inside was Neal. He reached out a hand to me. I'd never been so relieved to see anyone in my whole life ever. "Inside!" he commanded. I grabbed his hand. He pulled me in.

"Welcome aboard, my lady," said Lord Feathering, who was at the wheel. Neal pulled the door shut just as the thugs were pulling out handguns and beginning to fire at us. "How rude!" Lord Feathering commented calmly.

"Stop shooting!" I heard Edwin yelling. "We need her unharmed!"

Lord Feathering jammed the car into reverse. We shot backwards out of the destroyed office building, across its grassy front lawn, and back onto the road.

"Let's get out of here, shall we?" he said to me and Neal. He tore onto the main road, and we sped out of sight.

"And then the thugs grabbed me, and Edwin forced the blood sample from me."

I was sitting curled up on the red velvet sofa in the sitting room of Lord Feathering's manor. Lord Feathering had brought me a black fuzzy blanket, which I had wrapped around my legs for comfort. Neal was sitting opposite me on the sofa. Lord Feathering had disappeared to collect some things from his lab, and I was telling Neal all that had happened.

"That's jacked up," Neal said simply.

I shook my head thinking about it. "Edwin seemed like such a nice guy, too. But then he turned those thugs on me. It was just so horrible. Did you make progress on what Laboratory 735 was?"

Neal nodded. "Oh yeah. It took me a few hours, but I was able to hack into part of Globotek's system. It's crazy stuff. Honestly, Annie, I've never seen a civilian organization locked down as tight as that one is. As it stood, I was only able to access parts of their system, not the mainframe."

"You expected more?"

"From Feathering's lair, yes. His set-up downstairs is one of the best in the world. There's nothing he shouldn't be able to access down there. You've gotten yourself involved with some very dangerous people, Annie."

I pulled the blanket tighter around my body. "What do they want with me?"

"I promised I'd let Feathering share what we found," Neal said. "All I can say is I've been hacking into places since I was eight, and I've never seen anything like Globotek. These guys are serious about secrets."

A large woman with long, silver braids and wrinkled skin entered the room at that moment, followed closely by Lord Feathering. She was wearing a simple black dress and white apron and carrying a shiny silver tray of food, which she set on the fine glass coffee table next to me.

Lord Feathering politely introduced her. "Miss Annie, please meet Mrs. Westcott. Without a doubt, the most diligent and efficient cook I have ever employed."

Mrs. Westcott rolled her eyes. "He thinks this is high praise," she explained to me. "He thinks the joy of my existence is serving him cakes and tea. But I'll give him credit. He's the only gentlemen I've ever worked for who covers dental *and* retirement. Do give me a ring when the tea needs a refill." She indicated a small silver bell that was sitting on the serving tray. "You'll want to let it steep a few minutes before you pour." I nodded gratefully to her, and she disappeared back into the kitchen.

The teapot was silver, matching the tray. *Real* silver, I rather suspected. The teacups were fine china. Matching china plates held pieces of crumb cake and delicate silver forks. I reached for a plate and pulled it close to my chest, as if cake might give me the comfort I was looking for.

Lord Feathering helped himself to a plate and sat down opposite me in a high-backed, red velvet chair. Neal grabbed a slice of the cake, then moved to a matched red chair on the far side of the room. As he crossed the room, he pulled out his cell phone. "Ooh, I just heard back from Blossom," he said, tapping at the screen with one hand and juggling the cake and fork with the other. "She'll come straight here after she's done at work and not go back to our house for now."

"Good, good, good," nodded Lord Feathering. "No one will be able to give us problems in here. I've installed a rather unique security and defense system in the manor, Miss Annie. Even when Globotek does figure out where you've gone, there's no way they'll be able to get in."

I wasn't focused on his words. I stared at the piece of crumb cake on the end of my fork. The fork had a fine delicate pattern molded into it. I bit into the cake and was delighted by how tasty it was. Another bite gave me more courage. I sat up and poured myself some tea.

"So, Neal wouldn't tell me," I asked Lord Feathering, "*What* is going on?"

Lord Feathering nodded. The flirtatious air he had danced with yesterday was gone. He was all business and concern right now. He put down his cake and pulled out a small black controller. A large screen slid down from the ceiling. He tapped a few buttons.

A large picture of some kind of alien worm popped up onto the screen. It had a bunchy, blobby body that was long and segmented like a caterpillar. Eight awkward feet sprouted out from its body with three prong-like fingers on each. The face, if you could call it a face, had a puckered look, where the blobs of the body folded in upon itself. Which is really all to say... it was thoroughly and utterly gross.

"Ew!" I cried out. "What the heck is that thing?"

"That," said Lord Feathering, "is a tardigrade. Scientific name *Hypsibius dujardini*. Known informally as a water bear or moss piglet. It is about half a millimeter in length, and it is the most durable creature currently known to science. It can withstand temperatures as high as 300 degrees Fahrenheit and as low as -458. It can stay alive for ten years without food or water, withstand pressures greater than those found in the deepest ocean trenches, survive ionizing radiation at doses hundreds of times what would kill an average human, and survive the vacuum of space."

"Whoa," I said. "It sure is ugly." I finished my crumb

cake, put the plate down, and picked up my teacup.

"Miss Annie Glenn," continued Lord Feathering seriously. "I find it incredible to be telling you this, but your DNA has been fused with the DNA of this creature."

He paused to let the words sink in. I put the tea back down and sat up straight.

"I ran the tests three times to be sure," Lord Feathering continued. "And then Neal was able to crack into Globotek's research database, and we confirmed it. Globotek has been researching the genetics of tardigrades for the past fifteen years. Their goal has been to create a human super-soldier with the same physical capabilities and endurances as a tardigrade. It seems their founder Dr. Oswald Jaliswack has long had visions of creating an army of super-humans. What is of great concern to me personally is that he is not employed by any government and appears to be creating this army for his own personal benefit. It appears that Globotek recently perfected a delivery system which involves the simple breathing in of a virus that then immediately rewrites the DNA."

"The green gas in that weird room..." I whispered.

Lord Feathering nodded at me. "It's quite ingenious really. It would completely revolutionize the medical world of genetic manipulation. But he does not appear interested in marketing the technique. He is hoarding it for himself, ensuring that he is the only power on Earth capable of creating his super-soldiers. In fact, we rather think he is a...

oh, what was that phrase you used, Neal?"

"Egomaniacal madman intent on world domination," Neal chimed in, his face still buried in his cell phone.

"Yes, yes, that's right. Egomaniacal madman intent on world domination. And you, my dear Miss Annie, appear to be his first successful test subject. That was the project that Laboratory 735 was working on. The first successful integration of tardigrade DNA into that of a human."

I gulped.

"And it is even more than that," he continued. "A tardigrade can withstand temperatures of up to 300 degrees. Fire burns at a minimum of 480 degrees, but can rage up to 1500 degrees or more. A tardigrade would not have survived the building exploding, nor would it be able to hover contentedly in the middle of an open flame. So somehow, they have managed not just to harness the powers of a tardigrade, but to amplify them as well."

I held up my hands and turned them over in front of me. I still looked normal. But what had I become?

"So, what does that mean for me?" I asked quietly. "What does that mean I can do?"

"That, my dear Annie," replied Lord Feathering, "is what I hope, with your permission, to discover."

April 12th

My new reality began the next morning. I had been overwhelmed yesterday, and we had spent the rest of the day settling in. Blossom arrived around dinnertime, demanding to know what was going to happen to all the stuff left at our house, as none of us had exactly packed for this when we'd left the house that morning. Lord Feathering made a phone call and arranged for some burglars to break into our house and pick up our necessities. Our belongings would be secreted to us bit by bit over the next week or so, through various means and avenues. Too much activity at any one time might draw attention to the manor, and the longer we could conceal my whereabouts from the seeking eyes of Globotek, the better.

I remembered Edwin's words to me that I was *the breakthrough they'd been waiting for*. He'd called me *the woman who was going to save our world*. I realized that if Laboratory 735 was destroyed in the fire, then so was most of their research, and they wouldn't have the ability to just find another volunteer to zap. They needed *me* in a very real way. They would most certainly come looking. Scary thought!

Lord Feathering's manor had countless rooms, all decorated in ornate, antique fashion. I picked a bedroom on the second floor with a blue velvet king-sized bed. It had a canopy and thick curtains that could be drawn around the sides. The room had its own fireplace with a white fur skin rug laid out in front of it. The windows were tall and grand and overlooked the rear grounds of the estate. I could stand at the window and see a high-walled living maze, a rose garden, and a duck pond. This place was straight out of a fantasy novel, with Lord Feathering at the center of it all, pledging his allegiance to protecting me. I felt more safe and secure than I had in years.

Neal had picked a room down the hall from me. He was enjoying the change in circumstances. And indeed, as long as he had an internet connection, his life was not much interrupted. He worked from home in his tech support job, and he spent most of his free time gaming. He was happy as a clam to have access to the manor and its technology.

Blossom was significantly less enthusiastic about her newfound entrapment. We agreed that Globotek would not hesitate to use either of my roommates to find me, and so we didn't think it was safe for any of us to leave the manor grounds. Despite her dislike of her uncle, Blossom agreed. It was decided that her employer would be told that she had to leave town unexpectedly to care for her father, whom she would say had been in an auto accident. The Family Medical Leave Act would guarantee her up to three months of time away from the job. Since she hated her job anyway, she didn't mind the idea of abandoning it on short notice, but she couldn't stand the idea of being cooped up in her uncle's manor. She picked the bedroom next to Neal's and disappeared into it with a growl.

We did a review of other people whom Globotek might think could find me. My parents had passed away; I had no siblings or relatives. I had just moved to this town a few months back and had no significant friends or boyfriends to speak of. A little depressing to think about it that way, but everything was covered.

So it was that I awoke the next morning into my new reality with a blue velvet comforter wrapped around me. I pulled the curtain of the bed aside and let the sun shine in on me. My clothing had not yet arrived, but Lord Feathering had several closets of clothing to choose from. Mrs. Westcott had delivered everything that was in my size over to my room. It seemed that Lord Feathering was prepared for all manner of company and eventualities. I couldn't imagine how he had ended up with all this stuff, but I was certainly grateful that he had. My bedroom had its own private bathroom with a claw-footed tub next to a large window. It felt silly and luxurious to bathe naked next to an open window. But I drew up a bubble bath and giggled the whole time.

I picked through the clothing he had provided me with. Most of it was decades out of fashion. I found a pair of brown corduroys, which likely dated from the 1970s, and a free-flowing, blue, flowered shirt. It irked me that I had no makeup on hand. I struggled in front of the mirror to make my hair look attractive. Finally, I gave up and threw it into a small loose ponytail. It would have to do.

I left my bedroom, descended the grand staircase and, after a bit of wandering, found the dining room. Mrs. Westcott had served up a wonderful breakfast of apple walnut pancakes and blueberry yogurt parfaits. Blossom was at the table with a scrumptious plate in front of her.

"Good morning!" I smiled at her. I took a seat at the table and piled a plate high with apple walnut pancakes, dousing them in butter and syrup.

Blossom looked at me suspiciously. "Have you already had coffee this morning? I've never seen you so awake in a pre-coffee state before."

I poured myself some tea that was sitting on the table and grinned. "I just feel like I'm on this luxurious vacation in some crazy resort place. This place is fabulous!"

Blossom shook her head. "I'm happy you're happy,"

she grumbled and took a bite of blueberry parfait.

I realized I was being insensitive. "Blossom," I told her. "I know you don't like it here. And I feel really bad that you have to be here because of me."

She shook her head. "It's not your fault. Those crazy Globotek guys have hijacked all our lives. And frankly, I don't mind having a break from that job of mine. I'm so tired of running reports for a company that never even reads them."

"You thinking of quitting?" I asked her. I slurped my tea and stuffed a sticky wad of pancake into my mouth. It was *heavenly*.

Blossom nodded. "I need something new. Something I can get my heart behind. Something that matters, you know?"

"I want to be a hairdresser," I told her helpfully.

Blossom smiled. "I was thinking more of something in the non-profit world. Or international politics. I might take my temporary entrapment here as an opportunity to do some reflecting on that."

It made me happy to hear that. "I hope you find what you're looking for," I told her. "Pass the blueberries, will you?"

She handed me the blueberries. We continued chatting over our yummy breakfasts. Lord Feathering appeared just as we were finishing up.

He was dressed more casually than I'd seen him yet —

deep purple dress pants, a white shirt and paisley, purple velvet vest. He wore no tie, and his sleeves were rolled up, ready for work.

"Miss Annie," he greeted me with a smile. His bright blue eyes fixed on me and sparkled with excitement. He extended a gentlemanly hand. "Shall we begin?"

I blushed, took his hand, left my dirty plates at the table, and followed him. We descended to his underground laboratory. He led me deep into the lab. I hadn't realized before that the lab was so big. We passed strange machine after strange machine.

"What *are* all these gadgets?" I asked him as we walked.

"My inventions," he explained. "And my grandfather's too. He owned this manor and the lab before me, so much of the work is his."

"What kind of inventions?" Every single contraption we passed seemed to catch my eye.

Lord Feathering paused in front of one of them. "This is one of my most recent successes. I just finished building it last spring," he said. "Watch!"

I leaned down next to him. The machine looked simple enough. It had a single hard drive attached to two small platforms. He took off his watch and placed it on one of the platforms. He carefully checked the dials and hit a single button. A shimmering yellow light engulfed the watch. The light sparkled and disappeared, and the watch was gone. A second later, another shimmering yellow light danced and shone on the opposite platform. When that light evaporated, the watch sat resting on the second platform.

"It's a parlor trick!" I cried in amazement.

"I assure you, Miss Annie," he said, "it is a genuine matter transporter. The first of its kind. Must say, I'm rather proud of it. But we are getting distracted."

He led me further into the lab until we came to another machine. It stood ten feet tall and held a circular glass container tall enough for a person to stand in.

"This is my own personal version of a barometric pressure chamber. While you are inside, we should be able to simulate the pressure of being under the ocean or being in the vacuum of space. I have modified it such that we can test out sub-freezing temperatures as well. We will begin slowly and keep it simple. You have green, yellow and red buttons inside the chamber. I will adjust the chamber one notch at a time. At each increment, you will press a button. Green will indicate that you are feeling fine and ready to proceed. Yellow will tell me that you are feeling not great, but that you are comfortable trying the next level of pressure or temperature. The red button will tell me to stop and return the chamber to normal."

As he spoke, he began attaching various sensors to my body. "These will monitor your life signs," he explained. "If they give me feedback that concerns me, I will pull you out of the chamber even if you think you're feeling fine."

He secured one of them to the back of my neck. He handed me two to attach to the front of my chest, and he attached two to my back. I blush to admit that I enjoyed the professional touch of his fingers against the skin of my back. Were his fingers lingering on the skin of my back a second longer than was necessary? I must have imagined that. I felt lucky to be in the care of such a powerful man.

Test runs indicated that the machine and sensors were all working properly. I stepped into the chamber. The door slid shut. The experiments began.

Late that night, the first raid came. I woke up in my blue velvet bed to the sound of a loud crash. I rushed out into the hall and found Lord Feathering already there. Neal and Blossom were coming out of their rooms, too.

"Not to worry, not to worry," Lord Feathering assured us all. "That's just the manor's self-defense system kicking in. My guess would be that Globotek has found out where you're staying and is trying to get inside."

"That didn't take long!" Blossom was horrified.

Neal put his arm around her. "Well, we figured it wouldn't."

"Shall we take a look?" Lord Feathering said cheerfully. He led us up to one of his libraries on the third floor, which held the giant windows overlooking the front of the manor. The four of us stood together looking out. It was about a hundred yards to the wrought-iron fence that ringed the perimeter. As we watched, we could see men in SWAT gear hopping the fence and dashing across the grounds toward the manor. When they came within about fifty yards of the manor, the men became engulfed in yellow shimmering lights. They glowed and sparkled brilliantly, then vanished.

Neal, Blossom, and I all gasped.

"Works perfectly!" Lord Feathering cried delightedly.

"What happened to them!?" Blossom demanded.

"Nothing harmful, my summer flower," Lord Feathering replied happily. "They were simply transported off the manor grounds."

"The transporter you showed me in your basement?" I asked in awe.

He beamed with pride. "The one downstairs is just the

prototype. Fully functional, but operates only on a small scale. What you are seeing is the second version in action. I integrated the transporter technology into my manor's security sensors. When anyone attempts to approach the manor while the security system is on, they are identified as intruders and simply transported off the property!"

"Where are you sending them?" Neal watched the shining yellow lights in awe.

"I can pick the place at will. Tonight, they are being sent to a quarry just a couple miles down the road. Big open spaces are always best, especially when there are multiple transports involved. But if I wanted to, I could send them to the back country of Australia. Or even the moon!" He squealed in delight. "This is the first time I've ever gotten to see it in action. It's such a delight to watch!"

We watched the SWAT men disappear in shimmering yellow lights for a few minutes more. Then, one by one, we returned to our bedrooms and bid each other goodnight.

April 19th

I spent most of the next week in the chamber. The work was slow going. Despite my assurances that I was up for it, Lord Feathering refused to push my body in increments too large at any given time. But after seven days, we finally had some results. My body was fine in pressures greater than you would find at the bottom of the deepest ocean. I didn't start to feel the cold until -600 degrees Fahrenheit, and it remained unclear how cold it would have to get before I would actually suffer damage or freeze to death. I pleaded with Lord Feathering for us to keep going until we found out, but he flat out refused to risk it.

We were excited to try the effects of radiation on me. Lord Feathering needed just a few more parts to arrive before he could finish building the testing apparatus that he would need.

I delighted in working with him each day. He paid me

so much respect and care. His bright blue eyes twinkled with excitement in my presence. There was an energy alive between us – one that I enjoyed quite a lot.

And, every night, there would be some attack on the house, which would inevitably be thwarted by Lord Feathering's defense systems. I would draw the curtain on my blue velvet bed, wrap myself in my blankets, and fall peacefully asleep.

On the evening of the 19th, we joined Blossom and Neal in the dining room. They were in the middle of a scrumptious dinner of roasted lamb, potatoes and asparagus. Mrs. Westcott was truly a fabulous cook.

"What I don't understand," Neal was saying, "is what good is it?"

"How do you mean?" I asked.

"The tardigrade as a means of making a super-soldier. It doesn't add up," he replied. "Think about it. You can withstand explosions, which is certainly useful for a solider, but your other powers don't help in a standard battle. Who needs to withstand pressure to win a war? Any normal enemy would just shoot you. A tardigrade can't withstand a bullet. I assume you can't either."

"I was thinking the same thing," chimed in Blossom. "Remember when she got cut with the knife? Physically speaking, a knife functions similarly to a bullet. I'd bet a bullet would go right through her. And she doesn't have any special healing powers that we've observed."

The discussion soon veered off in a different direction, but the notion upset me. I left the dinner table early, feeling the need to clear my head. I went for a walk on the rear grounds of the manor. I wandered aimlessly through the rose garden and finally perched myself down by the duck pond.

What was the point of a super-soldier who could just be shot and killed? I wondered.

Edwin had called me *the woman who was going to save our world.* He certainly hadn't seemed concerned about bullets when he said it. What did he know that I didn't know? I wondered if Globotek had a super-armor suit all ready for me that would protect me from bullets. I kicked myself for getting into this situation in the first place. I swore to myself I would never sign anything ever again without reading all the fine print.

Had Edwin *really* told me everything on that tour he gave me? I certainly didn't remember him saying anything about super-soldiers or egomaniacal madmen with visions of world domination. But I did have him tuned out pretty effectively....

I suddenly wished everything could go back to normal. I looked at my hands. They looked so ugly. Sure, they were pretty on the surface, but just underneath they were infested with that disgusting worm DNA. I was a mutant.

A freak of nature. And it was my own stupidity that had gotten me here....

What *had* Edwin meant...? *The woman who was going to save our world?* I looked up from the duck pond. The sky was clear and a beautiful deep blue. Stars were just beginning to come out. Maybe I could just run away. Walk off the manor grounds and skip town. I could find a new town far away, get a new name. I could find some man to take care of me, and I could go to beauty school. I imagined myself in some unknown town, giving some teenager a perm for her prom or showing an elderly lady a new hairstyle that would hide her thinning hair. I'd hear all the gossip of the town and tell the young women that they should leave those jackasses who treated them so badly.

I looked at my hands again and was pulled back into reality. What on Earth was happening to me? I was a useless mutant, a would-be super-soldier who could be shot with a bullet on sight. And I had an international multi-corporation hunting me for my DNA.

At least I had a protector in Lord Feathering. At least in this manor, I was safe.

April 20th

Lord Feathering spent the day alone in his laboratory. Delighted that the awaited parts had arrived sooner than expected, he was hard at work building the apparatus that would test my tolerance for radiation. At dinnertime, a very busy Mrs. Westcott sent me downstairs with a tray to bring him a hot bowl of soup, warm buttered roll, and a cup of tea.

I balanced the tray carefully as I descended the secret stone staircase, not wanting to spill a drop. Lord Feathering's attention was engrossed in his network of computers. His multiple screens were alive with scrolling data and complicated graphics. He was wearing his normal work outfit – dark purple pants, white button-down shirt with the sleeves rolled up, and the deep purple vest. His back was to me, and I didn't want to disturb him.

"Your dinner is here," I said quietly.

He turned around, and his eyes sparkled when he saw

me. "Miss Annie," he said with a soft smile. "I wasn't expecting you."

"I brought you your dinner," I repeated and turned to leave him to his work.

"No, stay," he said. "Have a seat." He extended a hand, indicating some chairs to the side of the network. "I have been looking for a chance to speak with you more."

I blushed and took a seat.

"I feel I know more of your DNA than I know of you," he said, as he took the bowl of soup and began to eat. "Tell me a story. Tell me about yourself."

I blushed again, feeling on the spot and not knowing what to say. I pulled my feet up onto the chair, readjusting my short skirt for modesty. As I moved, my loose-fitting shirt slipped off my shoulder. I pulled it back into place and pushed my bra strap back under the fabric.

"I want to be a hairdresser someday," I told him.

He smiled. "Really?" he sounded delighted. "Tell me why!"

So, I started talking. I told him about how I'd taken a couple classes at a community college after high school, but I'd had to go to work full-time to make ends meet. Receptionist jobs were easy to get and paid a good wage for no college degree. But really what I wanted was to go to beauty school. I wanted to spend every day making women look beautiful. I just needed to save up the money to pay the tuition.

I told him more, too. It had been so long since anyone had asked me about myself that once I got going, it was like my whole life came pouring out of my lips. I told him about the kittens I had when I was a little girl, the spelling bee that I won in 5th grade, and the trip I took to Disneyland when I was ten.

He listened to me with an entranced look in his face. When he had finished his dinner and tea, he led me up out of the laboratory and then led me on a walk through the manor. He took me far down into the south wing – an area I had not yet explored. As we walked, I told him more stories. I told him about my parents, how they died in the accident six years ago, and how the Jenkins family had taken me in while I finished out my senior year of high school. I told him how I'd spent the next five years working as a receptionist in my hometown. I even told him how I'd dated Jimmy Houser for a while and what a sweet boy he was – the first boy I'd ever dated. Lord Feathering looked at me with his bright blue eyes. I smiled back.

"So, tell me about yourself," I said to him.

"There's nothing to tell," he shrugged. "I was raised in this house and have lived here my whole life."

He opened a set of double doors, and we stepped into a ballroom. My breath caught in my mouth as I took it in. The ceiling towered high overhead. Crystal chandeliers hung from the ceiling. There was a balcony with golden pillars. Tapestries adorned every wall, and moonlight streamed in through a long row of twenty-foot tall windows. It felt like a fairy tale. I had never been anywhere so spectacular.

"How can you say there's nothing to tell!" I exclaimed. "This manor is incredible!"

"It has its beauty, yes. And this is one of my favorite rooms. But its empty walls have grown dreary as of late. I like the spunk and color you have brought inside." He reached his hand up to my cheek and touched it softly.

This man never let up in making me blush. Slightly uncomfortable, I walked away from him, over to one of the windows. I looked outside at the moon and the clear night sky.

Lord Feathering walked with me. While I stood at the window, he stepped in close. I had never stood so close to him before. I realized for the first time that even though he was lean, he was quite muscular and solidly built. He stood six or seven inches taller than me. I felt awkward and small next to him.

"Miss Annie," he said, turning to face me. "If I may be so bold, I believe you are as beautiful as a work of art. I find I can no longer control myself around you."

Before I knew what was happening, he wrapped his arms around my waist, pulled me close to him and kissed me. I was surprised and flattered and flustered and shocked. I reached up my hands to push him back. He was a good man, yes, but he was old enough to be my father!

But Lord Feathering was strong and would not let me go. He held me tighter and continued his kisses.

"Miss Annie," he whispered at my ear. "Do not fight this. I know you want this, too."

He pushed me back against the wall, his whole body leaning into me.

"Lord Feathering," I began, but the words stuck in my throat. I could say nothing. He pushed his hand up under my shirt and began grasping at one of my boobs.

"Please, stop, stop," I sputtered. "Stop what you're doing!"

He paused and whispered in earnest. "I know that you don't mean that. I've seen it in your eyes. You've wanted this from the moment we met." Then he kissed me so forcefully that I had trouble breathing. I tried again to break away from him, but he would not let me go. His grip was too strong.

"You're hurting me!" I cried. His body pressed against mine. And, suddenly, I could feel it against me... the pulse of an erection through his clothing. I looked into his fierce blue eyes and saw the intensity and determination in his face. A wave of terror ran through me as I realized what he intended to do. I started screaming for help as loudly as I could.

Then right in front of me, an awful smile crept across his lips. "And, tell me, Miss Annie, who will hear your cries from this far into the south wing of the manor? We are alone here, you and I."

In one horrible and terrifying instant, I realized I'd been tricked. He had brought me to this isolated area of the manor on purpose, knowing exactly what he planned to do. He had tricked me into coming along. I felt like a fool. I felt terrified.

Tears began to form in my eyes. And I began to fight him. I flailed and kicked. He fought me back. In the struggle that ensued, he threw me onto the floor. The back of my skull hit the ballroom floor hard, and the world went black. When I could see clearly again, he was mounted on top of me. My clothing was ripped. He was leering down at me and running his hands across my skin. When I started to struggle again, he gripped my neck in the long fingers of his strong hands.

"Miss Annie," he commanded me, in a stern and angry tone. "I would not struggle if I were you. I would hate it if you forced me to cut off your air supply."

Why was he doing this? I'd thought that he would keep me safe.... I tried to push him away again, and he squeezed my throat with both of his hands until I sputtered and gasped for air. I froze every muscle then, afraid for my life. He relaxed his grip.

"That's better," he said with a chilling smile on his lips and a satisfied glint in his eyes. He kept one hand securely on my neck, pinning me down, while with his other hand he calmly began undoing his belt buckle.

I will write no more of what happened that night.

When he was done, he left me alone in the ballroom. I huddled against the window on the floor, curled up in a fetal position. All parts of my body were bruised and bloodied. Tears streamed down my face for hours. I did not move for a long, long time.

April 21st

I barely moved from my bed all the next day. I'd locked my bedroom door, praying that Lord Feathering did not have a key. I kept the drapes closed tight around my bed. I hid under my blankets. My body ached, and my head was pounding. For most of the day, I don't even know if my eyes were open or closed. It didn't matter. Whether my eyes were open or closed, I saw nothing but horrible images from the night before. I could still feel his hands touching me. I could still feel the weight of him on top of me. The scent of his hideous body would not go away.

I was dirty and used. I needed to get clean. I climbed fully clothed into the claw-footed bathtub and ran the water over me. I curled up in the tub and stared emptily out of the window. The water poured around me. It filled the tub, soaked my clothing, and tumbled back and forth. My fingers and toes grew wrinkled from the water. My entire body was drenched. But I couldn't get clean. I couldn't get clean. I couldn't get clean.

I dried myself off and threw the clothing away. I hid myself from the mirror when I walked by it. I got dressed again – slowly – in thick jeans and a black tee shirt. I had many bruises on my body, and it hurt to move. I crawled back into the bed and hid under the covers. I don't even know if my eyes were open or closed. It didn't matter. Whether they were open or closed, I saw nothing but images from the previous night.

At one point, Neal knocked on my door, asking if I was okay. I told him I was sick and was staying in bed. Mrs. Westcott knocked and left meals outside my door for me to eat, but I didn't bother to retrieve them.

When night fell, I heard a fresh batch of raiders outside. It was Globotek trying to find me again.

The decision was an easy one.

I got out of my bed and put on my black sneakers and black leather jacket. I packed a bag with a few changes of clothes, my teddy bear, journal, and some basic necessities.

Then, being careful that no one saw me, I snuck out of my bedroom, down the stairwell, and out the front door. In the fresh night air, I took off running. There was pain as I moved, but I didn't let it slow me down. I sprinted down the driveway to the wrought-iron fence. I felt grateful that the manor was designed to keep people out, not in. I slipped out the main gate and rushed toward the nearest men in SWAT gear I could find.

"My name is Annie Glenn," I called out to them. "Take me to Edwin Peabody."

April 22nd

The men in SWAT gear drove all night long. I fell asleep in the back of their van. I slept poorly. My dreams were filled with nightmarish images of Lord Feathering and the ballroom. I woke up when the van stopped at a drive-through for breakfast. I scarfed down three sausage, egg, and cheese sandwiches, two greasy hash brown patties, and a tall milk. It felt good to eat again, but my body still ached and my head was pounding. I lay back down again and closed my eyes, pretending to sleep until we arrived. I didn't like the dark images that filled my head when I did that, but I wanted to make small talk with the SWAT guys even less.

Our destination turned out to be another nondescript office building. They parked the van out front and led me in. The office room we entered was large and bright. It had the feel of an old newsroom from the movies. The main floor of the office was open, filled with desks and work stations. At each computer sat a miscellaneous employee in business wear. The place was a buzz of activity. When I entered, escorted by the SWAT team, the entire room hushed. All eyes watched us as we passed. We crossed the room, climbed a small spiral staircase, and entered a raised room with a wall of windows that overlooked the main floor.

Edwin Peabody sat at the desk, looking nerdy as always, but unusually meek. He wasn't wearing his white lab coat, but his suit and glasses were still ill-fitted and awkward. He stood when I entered, greeted me, and invited me to sit down. There were several matched armchairs in the room, all cushioned and comfortable. I picked the one where I could sit with my back to the wall.

He thanked the SWAT team for bringing me there. And to me, he asked kindly, "Annie, may I offer you some tea or coffee?"

"Coffee," I said instantly. The very idea of tea reminded me of Lord Feathering, which made me shudder and want to vomit.

Edwin signaled to an assistant on the lower level, who poured some coffee and brought it up to me. The SWAT team left, and Edwin closed the door.

He sat with me quietly while I drank my coffee.

"You have bruises on your neck," he said after a while.

I looked up at him. "Yes," I replied.

"And on your face. And on your arms."

"Yes," I replied again.

He was silent. "Are you in need of medical attention?" he asked presently.

I shook my head, which sent my headache into a rage. "I should say, though, I've got a wicked headache. I hit the back of my head a couple days ago, and it's been pounding ever since."

"I see," he nodded, then was silent. His thick-rimmed glasses began falling forward on his nose, and he nudged them back into place.

"Why did you come back to us?" he asked after a while.

I stared at the coffee cup, then looked up at him evenly. "I got to be honest with you, Edwin. I wasn't paying attention when you were talking to me on the tour. I didn't read a single word of the papers WorldPro had me sign. You all infused me with the DNA of a tardigrade, and I have absolutely no idea why. I can't feel heat. I can't be burned. I don't explode under any kind of pressure on Earth. But I can be kicked and punched and beaten and choked and cut and probably shot. Globotek is making super-soldiers, and I'm the breakthrough you've been waiting for. But what good is a soldier that can be overpowered as easily as me? You called me *the woman who is going to save our world*. I came back because I want to find out what you meant."

Edwin listened and nodded.

"I will answer your questions. And before we continue," he said, "I must first apologize to you with all my heart. We did believe that you knew what was happening and that you were a willing participant in the experiment. Furthermore, I must apologize for my behavior when we last met. I was under tremendous pressure from Jaliswack after the labs exploded. I was acting out of desperation, but that is no excuse. The action I took in forcing the blood sample from you was unconscionable, and I have spent every day since regretting it. You have my full assurance that you will not experience such treatment from me or from anyone employed at Globotek again, although I understand if my words carry little weight with you now. It is true that you are the first successful super-soldier that Globotek has created. And, as I'm sure you have realized, the destruction of the lab makes you also our only hope. As to why we need a super-soldier with the unique abilities of the tardigrade... I believe it will be easier for me to show you than it would be to explain it with words. I would ask you to please come with me."

I downed the last of my coffee and asked for a refill. Once the request was fulfilled, we left his office. Again, there was a hushed silence as his employees watched me walk through the main hall again and out to a series of elevators.

"Why are they staring at me?" I whispered to Edwin. "Is it because of who I am?"

"They have no idea who you are," Edwin whispered back, in a reassuring tone.

"Then why are they staring at me?" I repeated.

"Because with all your bruises, you look like you've been to hell and back!" he whispered back with the slightest of smiles on his face.

It hadn't occurred to me what I must look like. And arriving the way I had with all the SWAT guys... the businessmen must have thought the SWAT guys had beaten me up or something! The thought made me laugh. Then the laugh caused a rush of pain through my head that was so bad that I had to stop walking and cradle my head for comfort.

Edwin made a judgement call. "Our first stop will be the infirmary. Believe me, Annie. With what I'm about to show you, you're not going to want any distractions."

I nodded lightly my consent.

Edwin waved a key pass in front of a scanner. A green light beeped, and he pressed an elevator call button marked RESTRICTED.

"Everything I am going to show you from here on out is highly protected. There are only a handful of humans that have access to it and even fewer that have full knowledge of what actually happens here."

The infirmary was five floors up. It was clean and

comforting. At least, half of it was. The left side of the clinic was everything you'd expect. But the right side looked off. Way off. The beds were extra-long and wide. The medical tools were oversized and strangely shaped.

A nurse came and greeted Edwin and me. "Welcome! Do I have a new patient today? My name's Delphine, and I'll take right good care of you, sweetie."

She had a slight Southern accent and looked about a century out-of-date with her hair in a perfectly sculpted beehive over her head. Edwin wandered away to give me some privacy. Delphine smiled warmly as she asked how she could help.

I told her that I had hit the back of my head, and my head was raging. She did a scan of my head with a handheld tool and frowned sadly at the results.

"Sweetie, you've been through more than a blow to the head," she frowned. "You do have a concussion – that's easily dealt with. But I'm also seeing a lot of dysfunctional activity in the hippocampus and amygdala. Has anything traumatic happened to you lately?"

The question made me angry. "Don't get me started," I grumbled. "What kind of scanner thing *is* that anyway? Just give me the damn painkiller."

Delphine nodded kindly, ignoring my annoyance. She tapped a few more buttons on her scanner and did a second sweep around my head. Then she turned to her workstation and opened a cabinet door. Inside were dozens of vials containing powders of all colors. Each vial was numbered. She selected four separate vials, measured specific quantities from each, and mixed them together in a glass of water.

"Drink this," she told me. "It should put your brain back to rights."

I drank it down. Almost instantly, the pain subsided. The pounding stopped. I felt calmer inside, too. It was the strangest thing. I felt as if I could breathe more freely than I had in days. I felt as if all this sorrow and anger was suddenly lifted away from me. I closed my eyes, and, for the first time in two days, I didn't see threatening images of Feathering and the ballroom.

"Thank you," I said curiously. "What was that you gave me?"

"Compound 15732," Delphine replied in a reassuring tone, checking the readout on her scanner. "Each dose is mixed specifically to respond to the brain scan of the individual patient. It just arrived in the latest trade shipment. I mixed yours to heal the concussion and assist in healing some of the emotional trauma I observed in your brain as well." She glanced up at me kindly. "I hope you don't mind, sweetie."

I felt relaxed and happy. "No..." I said awkwardly. "Thank you...."

"It may not be a perfect fix. And it's certainly a new technology. I'd recommend you come back in a week or so for a follow-up evaluation."

I went back over to Edwin.

"Did she help?" he asked hopefully.

I nodded, still bewildered at how... *okay* I felt. Edwin grinned. It was the same endearing grin he'd had the first day I met him. I smiled back at him. We got back onto the elevator. He pulled out another key, inserted it into a small keyhole on the elevator wall, and turned it. A panel popped open, revealing a series of floor buttons that were labeled with symbols unfamiliar to me. He selected one of them, and we started going down.

"I'm sure you noticed as you drove up that this office building is built into the side of a mountain," he commented.

I hadn't.

"Much of that mountain was actually hollowed out to make this complex. It goes up about sixty stories inside the mountain and down deep into the mines underneath. Parts of the complex are still being built. We're going down to the mines right now."

A memory clicked in my head. "Neal said that Globotek did a lot of mining. We're at one of your mining sites now? Is that what we trade? That nurse mentioned trade shipments..."

Edwin began, "Globotek is a primarily a trade organization. We trade almost exclusively in raw ore. What sets us apart as a company is that we deal with a rather *unusual* set of trading partners."

"Neal couldn't figure out who you were selling to." I remembered.

"It's a highly protected secret. Not even the U.S. government knows who we trade with. I'll get back to that later. For the most part, we trade raw mined materials for amazing new technologies. The scanner you saw Delphine use and medical compound she gave you to drink are two examples of our latest acquisitions. Within a year, Globotek will be marketing those inventions to the world."

"Get to the part where you turn me into a super-soldier." I said.

Edwin hushed me. "I forgot to mention. The project Globotek was working on in Laboratory 735 was a highly protected project."

"You like that phrase, don't you?" I smiled. "*Highly protected...*"

He rolled his eyes and continued. "It is absolutely vital that the work at Laboratory 735 be kept secret from our trading partners. I was in charge of the project, and I reported directly to Oswald Jaliswack himself. Most of my employees didn't even know the full details of what we were working on and why, and, as you know, my entire staff was killed in the explosion. As of now, the only ones who know the project details from Laboratory 735 are myself, Jaliswack, you, and a small staff I have at a separate compound offsite."

"And those project details are?" I prompted him.

"The exact same details I told you when I gave you the tour at Globotek," he reminded me edgily. "But since you weren't *listening* the first time.... Our trading partners are an unruly sort. When they first arrived, there were all sorts of miscommunications and quite a bit of violence. We took a lot of casualties and couldn't find any way to oppose them militarily. It was Jaliswack who came to understand that they were just businessmen and could be dealt with as such. Over time, he was able to forge a peace with them and set up a mutually beneficial trade situation, which has continued for the past two decades with excellent success."

"And made Jaliswack tons of money in the process," I added cynically.

"And given the world access to a remarkable number of technologies that never would have been possible without him," Edwin said, "the likes of which I would never even have dreamed of in my earlier years as a scientist."

"Get to the part where I care about this," I prodded again.

"Our trading partners have been becoming more and more demanding about the terms of our trade. It used to be that our mining operations were sufficient for supplying them with the raw materials they requested, but they have recently demanded that they take over operating the mines themselves. They believed ore could be produced more efficiently and cheaply, if they were in charge. For us, this is unconscionable. But, as I have said, we have no physical means of defense against them. Jaliswack has had few options but to capitulate to their demands. That is, until now. Until you."

The elevator began to slow down, and Edwin spoke in a rushed and quiet tone to get everything in. "We are about to arrive at the mines, and you will see our trading partners overseeing current operations. Say absolutely nothing while you are on this floor, and do nothing to draw attention to yourself. I told you that our trading partners arrived from far away two decades ago. I need to be clear that they arrived from *very far away*."

The elevator doors opened. We stepped out onto the platform. I gasped.

We were on a small platform overlooking the pit of an active mine. A railroad track ran below us, and men with headlamps were at work all about, swinging tools and hauling rocks. In the center of the pit stood a group of... *creatures*. Creatures the likes of which I had never seen or ever even imagined.

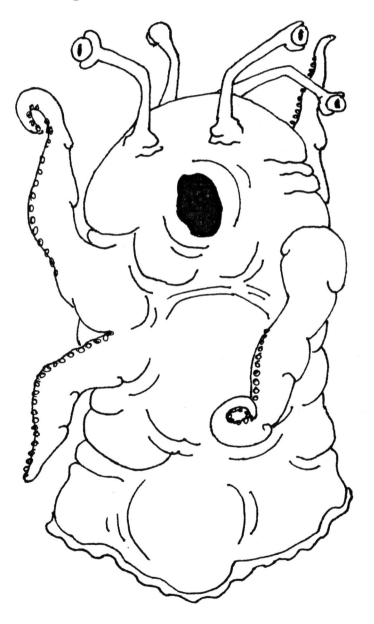

They stood about eight feet tall. Their bodies were bulbous, round, and gooey-looking – like gelatin. Their skin was a mottled mix of red, purple, and grey. They had four tentacled arms that flayed out about them, undulating and covered with suckers like an octopus. Their mouths were big gaping holes in the "fronts" of their bodies. They had no identifiable noses, lips, ears, or necks. Their eyes were the oddest features. Four thin stalks poked up from the tops of their rounded heads, an eyeball implanted at the end of each one. As they moved about, their eye stalks shifted and twisted, turning every which way and seeing in every direction at once. They had no legs. Their gelatin bodies simply blobbed out at the ground level. The bottoms of their blobs undulated and rolled such that they slid, rather than walked, across the floor of the mine.

"What are they?" I whispered in horror to Edwin.

He shushed me hurriedly. I could see fear in his eyes, and I kept silent. He whispered, "Their species is called the Marguar. They are from a planet in a neighboring galaxy."

One of the creatures held a bullhorn up to his face and shouted into it. I could hear the noises he made – a cacophony of burps, bellows, and grunts. But from the other side of the bullhorn, commands barked out in the English language. "KEEP MOVING! KEEP MOVING!" he was yelling. "YOU'RE FALLING BEHIND ON PRODUCTION. THERE'S TWO MORE CARTONS TO FILL IF ANYONE WANTS TO EAT TODAY!"

As he spoke, he lifted a bullwhip in one of his tentacled arms. With a loud crack, he whipped it at one of the nearby miners. The man screamed and fell to the ground. I gasped and Edwin squeezed my shoulder, warning me to stay silent. I held my breath and kept watching. Blood gushed from the man's back. The other miners, instead of hurrying to help, rushed away from him and swung their tools faster and with more force. The Marguar slithered over to the bleeding man and bellowed through his bullhorn.

"THIS MAN HAS FALLEN BEHIND ON HIS WORK! HE IS BEING MADE AN EXAMPLE OF. SEE TO IT THAT YOU ARE NOT NEXT!"

With a third tentacle, the Marguar pointed a strange, black gun at the man and fired. A red light shot out of the weapon and hit the man. His clothing and body burst into flames. There were a few seconds of agonizing screams. Then silence. From our platform above, I could smell the sickening stench of charred flesh. The Marguar grunted a few commands to its companions and slithered away. Three other Marguars instantly attacked the dead body, tearing it limb from limb, gnawing the cooked flesh off the dead man's bones, and slurping down his organs.

I was going to vomit. I turned to Edwin and pulled at his sleeve in desperation, afraid to make a noise lest we be discovered. He rang the elevator door, which thankfully opened instantly. He pulled me inside the compartment.

The shiny doors shut. I collapsed to my knees and retched onto the elevator floor.

"What the hell was that!" I screamed when my stomach was finished. I curled up into a seated position on the floor of the elevator and looked up at Edwin.

Edwin shook his head sadly. "I am sorry you had to see that," he replied. "I didn't know that *that* was going to happen. But I also think it is good that you understand the true nature of our situation. You have seen firsthand the reason for our desperation. You and I are going to leave this complex now. We have already been here longer than is wise."

"The miners...." I whispered. "Who are those people down there? This is America! Those people have families! Rights! There are laws!"

Edwin sighed. "Yes and no," he replied. "Because of the nature of our trading partners, Jaliswack has been very selective about who he uses in the mines. I do not personally approve of this portion of Jaliswack's business practices. I'd rather prefer to pretend it isn't true. But I am committed to being honest with you, Annie. You deserve to know all of the truth."

"And that is?"

"Most of the men down there are from other countries; they entered this country illegally and Jaliswack picked them up. In some cases, he arranged for them to be transported here from their home countries into ours. They live in the sixty floors above us in the mountain complex. At Jaliswack's orders, they are not allowed to leave."

I shrank in horror. "He's a slaver!"

Edwin did not disagree. "It is safe to say that not one miner knew what he was getting into when he came here. But ever since the Marguars took over the mine, it's gotten even worse for them. Jaliswack had never physically beat them, and he had always ensured that they were well fed."

"That doesn't make his behavior excusable."

"No, it doesn't," Edwin agreed. "I am merely trying to give you the most accurate information that I can. Jaliswack doesn't like how the Marguars have been treating the miners, either. He is doing all in his power to control the aliens, but, as I said, we have little bargaining power at this point."

I was slowly putting it together. "Jaliswack is in over his head with the aliens. And if he goes to the government for help, then he risks getting arrested himself."

Edwin nodded. "Human trafficking and slavery. He likes to phrase it differently, of course, but in a word, yes. It is good for you to understand this, Annie. However, even if he did go to the government, even they wouldn't have weapons that could work against the Marguars."

"Oh, come off it," I said. "They're the government! They must have tons of weapons that could kill these aliens."

"I used to work for the military," Edwin told me.

"Okay, that surprises me," I admitted.

The elevator doors opened onto an underground parking lot. We exited, and Edwin led the way to his car.

"The peculiar composition of a Marguar's physical body is resistant to any of the weapons that humans have invented thus far. When they first arrived on Earth, as I said, there were clashes. We found that human weapons had very little effect on them. Bullets go right through them. Blowing them up doesn't kill them. It divides them. A Marguar can regenerate its body from even the smallest bit of tissue. You blow a Marguar to a thousand pieces, and you literally end up with a thousand Marguars."

Edwin's car turned out to be a beige Volvo. He held the passenger door open for me, and I stepped in. The back seat was cluttered with notebooks, papers, and empty cans of peach-flavored sparkling water. From the rear-view mirror hung a small plastic astronaut with a hula skirt on. It made me smile.

"We have nukes," I argued back to Edwin, as he climbed into the driver's seat.

"Yes," Edwin agreed. "And if we wanted to irradiate the better part of this good state, I'd be all for nuking this entire complex, except for the part where we'd be slaughtering hundreds of innocent enslaved miners. Plus, don't you think the American public would prefer it if we *didn't* set off a nuke in their backyard? We are less than ten miles from several cities here. No, nukes cannot be a solution. We need to beat them in hand-to-hand combat. And we need to do it soon. It was a couple of months ago that they took over the mine. But now, they are demanding even more from us."

"How much worse could this possibly get?" I asked incredulously, as we sped away. I couldn't help but notice that Edwin seemed to be leaning on the accelerator a little harder than was strictly necessary. I suspected I wasn't the only one who was jittery after what we'd just witnessed.

"The Marguars have informed us that their interests in Earth now extend beyond running a simple mine or supporting a trade with humans. Their new plan is an on-Earth settlement for their species. They aim to colonize the planet and enslave humanity. And, as I said, we have no viable defenses against them."

"WHAT!" I screamed.

"Their first ship of colonists is already on its way. It is set to arrive within weeks."

"I think I need to puke again."

"And that, Annie, is where you come in. I told you that not even the strongest bullets can do much damage to them. What they *are* susceptible to is temperature."

"The tardigrades..." I whispered. It was suddenly all coming together.

"Now, you see," he nodded. "The Marguars are weakest where tardigrades are strongest. For us to create a fighting force capable of stopping them, we need to be strongest where they are weakest. And we need to be able to withstand their weapons."

"Which are?" I asked nervously.

"Heat rays and freeze rays."

"Oh!" I said brightly. "Well, that's no problem!"

For the first time that day, Edwin's face brightened into a smile. "And *that*, Annie Glenn, is why you are the breakthrough that we have been waiting for. That's why *you're* the woman who is going to save the world."

Edwin and I arrived at our destination sometime past midnight. He had driven all afternoon, and I wondered if we were in a different state again. I couldn't say for sure. I had fallen asleep in the car, gotten distracted with my journal writing, and generally failed to pay attention. Our destination was a large compound in the middle of nowhere. Edwin explained that this was where the resistance was housed. He didn't call it "the resistance," but that's because he's a nerd-scientist type. Me, I figure if you're putting together a secret group of fighters and technicians who are all bent on overthrowing and destroying an invading alien species, then that's a resistance.

The compound was extensive. Edwin promised a tour in the morning, but I did notice what looked like a cafeteria as he showed me the way to my new bedroom. The room he set me up in was small and dingy. The bed was a surplus army mattress on a squeaky cot.

He apologized for the crudeness of it all. I told him I'd just seen a bunch of aliens eat a human being. I could handle crude if it meant getting them off our planet.

Edwin bid me goodnight and left me to settle in. I unpacked the few belongings I'd brought along. I sent a text to Blossom and Neal to let them know that I was well, that I was with Globotek, and that they were free to leave the manor and resume their normal lives. Almost immediately, I got texts back loudly demanding explanations. I said I'd tell them more later, but it seemed that Globotek wasn't as evil as we thought it was. *Well*, I thought about the enslaved miners, *Globotek is still pretty evil, but an invading alien species bent on enslaving humanity kind of trumps human-to-human slavery. At least for now.*

I changed into the pajamas I'd brought, crawled into my uncomfortable, squeaky bed, hugged my teddy bear tight, and couldn't sleep. I thought about how desperate Edwin had been when he'd forced the blood supply from me. His behavior had not been cool. His apology had meant a lot to me this morning. And now I really understood what he had been so desperate about. I wondered if I wouldn't have done the same thing in his shoes.

I stared at the dusty ceiling above me and thought about the men in the mine – not just the man who had been killed – but all of them. Most of them had looked

Hispanic or Asian. Where did each of them call home? What lives had they been taken from when Jaliswack enslaved them? I lay in bed awake for a long time, thinking about the man I'd seen die this afternoon. Would his family ever find out what happened to him?

Globotek brought me here to save the world from the Marguars. But who would save those men from Globotek?

April 23rd

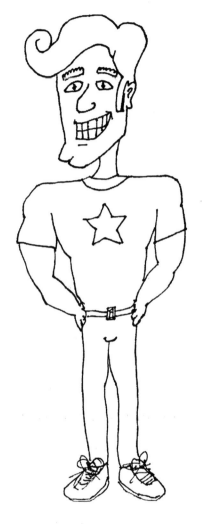

This morning, I began my crash course in saving the world. The mission was simple. I would be a member of a SWAT team. We would fly into space, board the Marguar, download as much information from the ship as we could (so that we could learn as much as possible about our new enemies), and then blow the ship to smithereens while making our dashing escape.

The leader of the team was a guy named Chip. He was the kind of guy who could be the hero of his own movie. He was 6'4", muscular, with bright blond hair, a constant shiny smile, and a cleft chin. The three other members of the team all seemed miscellaneously interchangeable with one another. They were all about 5'11", had short, brown hair, and looked generically handsome and tough. These were the kind of guys who did pull-ups for fun. Their names were Rod, Todd and Dodd.

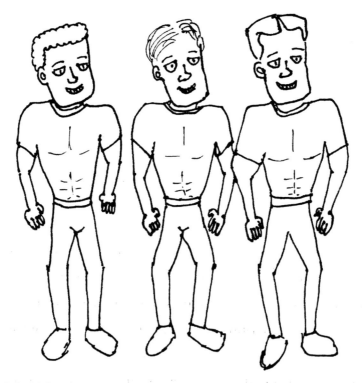

If Laboratory 735 hadn't blown up, all the team members would have been genetically manipulated. (And I wouldn't have been here.) But since I was the test subject who happened to survive before the lab exploded, I was the only one who was impervious to the Marguar weapons. The guys would just have to make do. And we'd all save the world together.

This was going to be fun.

Our first stop was getting me my super-suit. They called it a "uniform," but it was made of material that would repel bullets and blades, so *I* called it a super-suit. I put it on and admired myself in the mirror. It covered my entire body from my neck, to my wrists, and down to my ankles. The suit was a deep blue with a light blue V pattern across the chest. It was thick, but comfortable, easy to move in, and rather flattering to my figure. Another person might have gotten hot in the bullet-blocking material, but I didn't get hot anymore. I felt incredibly sci-fi.

I asked Edwin if I could have a cape to go with my super-suit. He said I needed to be taking this more seriously.

"Now," Edwin continued, as I struck a superhero pose in front of the mirror, "the rest of the team's uniforms have similar bulletproof capabilities as yours, but yours has an extra capability that theirs don't have."

I struck a karate pose, facing the mirror. Then another.

"Since your body can resist freezing and burning temperatures, your suit has been constructed of a material that also will not burn up or freeze. Um, Annie, are you listening to me? This is important."

I was totally listening to him. "Why don't you give the guys the same kind of suit as me? Seems like they'd need it more than I do."

"The suit resists burning up by itself becoming superheated. You're the only one who can withstand wearing it without being roasted alive."

Hunh.

Now that I was super-suited up, Chip, Rod, Todd, and Dodd took me to the armory. Dodd gave me my tutorial in Marguar weaponry and defense technologies. Or maybe it was Todd. Or… Rod. I couldn't really keep them straight. By the end of the day, I was just calling them "the Odds". Chip was the only one I knew for sure.

The armory was a large room in the basement of the compound. It was stacked with a wide variety of automatic weapons. I recognized M16s, but not the rest. Most of the rest made the M16s look like matchsticks.

"A Marguar has an unusual worm-like body composition that is uniquely unresponsive to traditional human projectile weaponry," Dodd/Todd/Rod was saying. "Not even one of these weapons is effective in killing them. Whatever hole we poke in them or tentacle we blow off them will just grow back in a matter of seconds. What they *are* susceptible to is temperature. Heat rays and freeze rays. It's what they use to arm themselves, and we've managed to fabricate a few of our own, pirated from their technology."

Then Dodd (we'll say it was Dodd) came to a locked cabinet at the end of the armory. He opened it to reveal weapons the likes of which I had never before seen. There were maybe twenty weapons total – half of them black, the other half white. The black weapons seemed to each have four separate barrels – each slightly different in length. Instead of a bullet chamber, there was a round clear glass ball, about three inches wide. The white weapons each had a single barrel jutting forward, that ballooned out like a bell toward the end. Four long talons curled forth, circling around that central barrel. The weapons looked strange and gothic and curious.

Dodd grabbed a pair of gloves from the cabinet and pulled them on. Then he picked up one of the white weapons and held it up for me to see.

"This one's the freeze ray," he began.

Excited, I reached up and took it from him, being careful to keep the curly talons pointed away from both him and me.

"Hey, hey, whoa, wait!" he said. Then he trailed off into silence.

I turned the freeze ray over in my hands. It had a dual trigger system and fit comfortably in my small hands.

Suddenly, I noticed that Dodd was staring at me.

"What?" I asked him.

"You... um..." he began. "You're holding the freeze ray with your bare hands."

"And?" I suddenly wondered why he'd put the gloves on.

"It doesn't feel... *cold?*"

"Oh, is it cold?" I shrugged. "It's probably that tardigrade thing. I don't feel cold like you guys do."

Dodd nodded, dumbfounded. "Touching a freeze ray causes frostbite. We have to wear the gloves to protect our hands. Hey, guys! Check this out!" he called to the rest of the team. Then suddenly I had three Odds and a Chip all circled around me amazed that my skin wasn't frostbitten.

Oh, for Pete's sake.

The guys grabbed gloves and freeze rays, and we all headed over to a big open room that was set up like an obstacle course. Our training ground.

"You've fired weapons before, right?" Chip asked me.

I shrugged. "Rabbit hunting with my grandpa as a kid."

"The freeze ray works much the same as a handgun. No safety on these guys, though. Point and squeeze, and you'd better mean it when you do. Two triggers - two settings. The upper trigger is setting one. It encases your target in ice."

"Observe!" piped in one of the Odds, and he fired the freeze ray at a nearby punching bag. A blue beam shot out, sending out a ferocious white spray, making a noise that sounded for all the world like the steamer on an espresso machine. When the air cleared, the punching bag was encased in a solid block of ice.

"This is my new favorite toy," I told Chip.

"Yeah," he grinned. "Mine, too."

"Does that kill a person?" I asked.

"Nope," said Chip. "The water just melts off them in an hour, and they're none the worse for wear. That's the upper trigger in action. The lower trigger, though, that's setting two. Lethal to both Marguars *and* humans. Setting Two turns all the water inside a person's body into ice – cells and all. You freeze to death from the inside out."

The third Odd showed up with a raw piece of steak, fresh and dripping with blood. (Presumably he'd just taken a quick trip to the cafeteria. I hadn't noticed.) Chip shot it at setting two. When the air cleared, a frozen solid piece of meat was revealed.

Totally my new favorite toy.

We spent a couple hours running drills and playing on obstacle courses. We practiced, practiced, practiced with the freeze rays. At one point, Chip left on some errand, and I whispered to the Odds, "Don't you wonder what happens if I get shot with one of these things?" Before the guys could say anything, I used setting one on my freeze ray to shoot my foot. The guys screamed and tried to pull me away from the blast, but it was a useless gesture. The espresso steamer sounded, the white cloud cleared, and we looked. There was ice on the ground around my foot, but no ice had formed against me or my clothing.

I grinned. Within seconds, Dodd, Rod and Todd were all aiming at me and taking their best shots. Again and again, the freeze rays had no effect. After a while, we got up the courage to try setting two on me. I didn't even feel a chill.

"This is cool," I said, then giggled. "No pun intended."

Chip freaked out a bit when he walked in to see Rod shooting me in the face at point blank range, but he recovered when he saw I was okay. But Chip still made a rule that no one was allowed to shoot me anymore. Party pooper.

At the end of the day, I grabbed dinner in the cafeteria with the guys. We talked for hours about all kinds of crazy stuff. We were psyched to blow the alien spaceship out of the sky. I have never had so much fun in my life.

April 25th

Heat ray day.

I had much less of a taste for the heat rays. Having seen firsthand what they do to a human being, working with them made me a little sick to my stomach. It cheered me up a bit when I started pretending to be blasting Lord Feathering into a burnt and charred mass. And it made me feel even better when we all turned the heat rays on me and found that I was completely unfazed by them. It's a good feeling, you know. Being invincible and all that. I spent a lot of that training day pretending that I was scorching Feathering.

"The major limiting factor of the heat rays," Rod told me at some lecture point in the day, "is that they need to charge. You can only fire one a few times before it needs to rest and recharge itself."

"Bummer," I said.

"Marguars also have powerful self-defense shields,"

Chip added. "It's kind of like an energy barrier, which means that freeze rays and heat rays are only effective against them in close quarters. So, when you're fighting them, you'll need to get inside their energy barrier to shoot them. If you're more than ten feet away, the rays will just bounce off their shields."

"Bummer," I said again. I thought about that. Any of these guys would get burnt to a crisp or frozen solid long before they got within ten feet of a Marguar.

I sobered up for a moment. I realized that Chip, Dodd, Todd, and Rod were really going to risk their lives when we boarded that ship. They had no protection from these weapons and yet they were going anyway. I was beginning to like these fellows and really respect them, too. I swore to myself I'd make sure that every one of them came back alive. I wouldn't let any of them get hurt.

Later that day, I went for a walk outside. I passed by one of the Odds on the way out of the compound, and he invited himself to join me. Turned out it was Rod. We went outside and started exploring the grounds around the compound. It was an isolated area. Mostly all we found were grassy rolling hills. There wasn't much else for scenery. The sun was beginning to set, though, and the sky was lit up with shades of purple, orange, and rose. The hills shown pink in the evening light. And there was a warm wind coming across the hills. It was a plain kind of beauty. But it was nice.

"Can you believe there's really a bunch of aliens up there, planning to invade our planet?" I asked Rod, staring up at the sky as we walked.

Rod laughed and shook his head. "Isn't it just crazy surreal?" he agreed.

We talked about random things as we walked. Rod thought the heat rays were more fun; I preferred the freeze rays. The weirdest food he'd ever eaten was herring eggs; the weirdest I'd ever eaten was squid. I was an only child; he was the youngest of five brothers. My dream was to be a hairdresser; his was to backpack across the Australian outback.

Slowly, the colors in the sky faded into deep blue, and we headed back to the compound. Chip and the Odds all had their own crappy bedrooms in the same hallway as mine. I thanked my new teammate for the company and wished him goodnight. As I changed into my flannel pajamas and crawled into my uncomfortable army surplus bed, I thought how nice it was to be making a new friend. I had spent almost an hour alone with Rod, and he hadn't flirted with me once the whole time. I felt oddly relieved about that. I curled up with my teddy bear and fell fast asleep.

April 28th

Chip, the Odds, and I were starting off our morning with some heat ray target practice, when Edwin came in with a worried look on his face. Chip called a halt, and we gathered around Edwin.

"We're scrapping the mission," Edwin said mournfully. "There was a mishap in engineering. Major setback with the Defender. It will never be ready in time."

After the roar of disapproval from our team died down, I piped up, "What's the Defender?"

Dodd shook his head. "It's our spaceship. What happened to it?"

"The ship itself is fine. But the transport arm blew up."

"What's that mean?" I asked.

Todd's turn. "It's how we're supposed to get on board the Marguar vessel. The Defender flies in close, extends the transport arm, suctions onto the side of their vessel. Then we cross over to it, cut a hole in their ship and get on board."

Dodd again. "No transport arm. No way to get on the ship."

"We're scrapping the mission," Edwin repeated. "We'll have to wait until they land and then lead a ground assault."

"Didn't that go badly the last time?" I asked.

"Yes," Edwin nodded. "Very badly. And it certainly means the rest of humanity will find out about the aliens. We're already at work rebuilding the lab. We think we're only a couple months away from being able to create more super-soldiers."

"But they'll be here long before then!" I exclaimed. "We can't let those space-slugs run wild on our planet just because we can't get on board a stupid old spaceship!"

Edwin shrugged. His frustration was evident, but he was at a loss. My whole team erupted in complaints, spouting off one useless possibility after another. All at once, it clicked in my head, and I knew what we had to do. I got a sinking feeling in the pit of my stomach as I spoke up.

"We're not scrapping the mission." I spoke up over the din. "I got a way to get us on that ship. Get me back to that damned manor you found me in. The jackass who lives there has a transporter we're going to steal."

I texted Blossom to let her know we'd be coming by.

Well, technically, I said I'd be coming by. I let Chip and the Odds be a surprise. When we drove up to my house in the white van, we were dressed for battle. Crisp blue super-suits with shiny white freeze rays on our belts. I didn't have my keys anymore, so I rang the doorbell.

Blossom and Neal were speechless when they saw us. We piled into the house and promptly took over the living room. "Nice digs you got here!" Rod complimented me. I grinned at him and put a pot of coffee on. I did quick introductions, but offered no explanation to my roommates about who these guys were or why we were all dressed so funny. As Blossom and Neal remained speechless, I started in on why we had come.

"Blossom, we need you to text your Uncle Archie and tell him you need to come over tonight. He'll turn off his security system if he's expecting you. You can drive your SUV right up to the manor with all five of us in it. We need you to get us into that house."

When Blossom was still speechless, I turned to the team and kept going. "I'll lead the way once we get in the manor. The lab has tons of junk and stuff in it, but I'll know the transporter when I see it. There shouldn't be much resistance once we're inside. If we see a sweet little old lady in a maid's uniform, that's Mrs. Westcott. We don't want to hurt her. If Lord Feathering gives us any problems, though, we can hurt him."

Blossom finally got her wits together. "Annie, what is

going on? What have you gotten yourself into!"

I grinned at her. "Globotek turned me into a tardigrade super-soldier. We need to steal your uncle's transporter, so we can save the world from a colonizing spaceship of human-eating aliens."

I don't think she believed me.

"You should have a cape to go with that outfit," Neal said wryly.

"That's what I keep telling them!" I threw my hands up in the air.

"You're not getting a cape," Chip shook his head for the hundredth time.

Even though Blossom didn't believe our story, she was delighted to help us do something to annoy her uncle. She sent him a text, claiming she'd left some vital piece of makeup at the manor and needed to swing by and find it. He bought it and texted back that he'd have tea and cakes waiting. His reply made both of us cringe. But it was the news that we needed.

We piled into Blossom's SUV, and she drove us out to the manor. The sun was just beginning to set when she pulled in past the wrought-iron gate and drove up to the gargoyle-encrusted main door. The closer we got to the manor, the more I felt a horrible tightness in my chest. I didn't want to go inside. I wanted to curl up in a ball and hide. I wanted to run away. I shook my head fiercely to shake the panic away. Blossom parked in front of the three-headed dragon fountain.

She left us hidden in the car while she went up and knocked on the door. I let out a huge sigh of relief when Mrs. Westcott opened the door. Blossom stepped inside and motioned to us a thumbs-up. My team and I dashed up to the door, freeze rays in hand, and peered inside. Blossom was guiding Mrs. Westcott up the stairs with friendly chitchat. I motioned to Chip and the Odds, and we slinked into the house, shutting the twelve-foot-tall door behind us. The guys were gaping at the décor in the main hall. I remembered how impressed I had once been with it all as well.

Then suddenly, there he was.

Lord Feathering stepped out from one of the hallways and stood directly in front of me, clad in dark green and towering over me. My heart pounded. *Run!* my body screamed. I couldn't move.

"Miss Annie!" he exclaimed affectionately. "You've come back to me!" His manner was so welcoming and pleasant that it made me want to vomit. My brain flooded with unspeakable memories of him pushing his body against mine. I froze. I couldn't scream. I couldn't move.

Then suddenly, a blue beam shot out toward him and overwhelmed him in a ferocious white spray. When the air cleared, Lord Feathering was encased in a solid block of ice, and Chip stood at my side, holstering his freeze ray.

"That ice won't melt for an hour, but we should probably be out of here before your Mrs. Westcott discovers him in that state," he grinned at me.

I gasped and slowly realized that I was breathing again. "Uh..." I struggled to regain my senses.

"I trust that was the jackass you mentioned who owns this place?" Chip prompted me, motioning toward the frozen man.

I nodded dumbly.

"Very good," Chip clapped me on the shoulder. "Let's go get that transporter."

In less than ten minutes, Blossom, Chip, the Odds, and I were speeding away from the manor with the transporter safely stowed in the trunk. Chip and the Odds were squealing about how cool the inside of the manor was. They wanted to go back and try out all the inventions in the lab. They *really* wanted to try out all the weapons hanging on the walls. I was riding shotgun, and I stared emptily out of the window as Blossom drove us back to the house. We'd accomplished our mission. But the way I had frozen when I'd seen *him*... I felt like a failure. A scared little girl.

It was late when we got back to the house, so we decided to crash the night there. Blossom pulled out extra blankets and pillows, and we created four places for Chip and the Odds to sleep. The guys and Neal all crowded around the transporter and set in playing with it. "Don't break it," I warned them. "We need that thing working."

I said my goodnights and disappeared up to my bedroom. I wasn't tired. I just wanted to be alone. As soon as I closed the door of my bedroom, I was overwhelmed with the joy of being home. I put on my baby blue flannel pajamas and crawled into my bed, which seemed at that moment to be the absolute most perfect place in the whole world.

There was a soft knock on my door, and Blossom came in. I smiled and motioned for her to sit down.

"I saw what you guys did to my uncle," she said.

I suddenly realized that she might not appreciate us freeze-blasting her relatives. "It doesn't hurt him," I assured her. "The ice melts off in an hour, and he's none the worse for wear."

"I've never heard of a weapon that can do that," she said slowly. "You weren't kidding about the aliens, were you?"

I sighed and shook my head. "No. I wasn't kidding."

Then I told her all I'd seen since I had left the manor. I told her about Globotek and the Marguars, about the aliens in the mines and how I'd seen them burn and eat the miner. I told her about how there was an invasion coming, and they were planning to establish a colony of aliens on our planet, and how I was the only person on the planet who could withstand their weaponry.

I told her about Edwin and Jaliswack, the freeze rays and heat rays, and what my super-suit could do. I told her about training with Chip and the Odds, and how great the guys all were, especially Rod. I even told her my secret concern – that they would just get in the way when it came time for me to take on the Marguars. But I still really liked training with them. I was just determined that when the time came, I would keep them safe.

She kept shaking her head as she took it all in. "It's just so unbelievable," she kept repeating.

I had to agree.

"So, how are you, Blossom?" I asked her. "Have you had any more thoughts about your job?"

"Thanks for asking," she said. "I've basically started job searching. Not sure what I'm looking for, though. I'll know it when I find it, though. I hope."

"You'll do something awesome, whatever it is."

She smiled appreciatively. I thought for a second that she was going to get up and say goodnight. But instead, she got nervous and shy.

"Annie," she said, quietly. "I don't want to be nosy, but I need to ask. I don't know why you left the manor, but I'm sure that somehow it was Uncle Archie's fault. I wanted to say that if you wanted to talk about anything, I'm here."

I didn't like her asking that question. I looked away from her and studied my fingernails for a long time. My eyes started to brim with tears. I wiped them off, and even more tears took their place. Blossom scooted over next to me and gave me a hug. When I felt her comforting arms around me, I burst out sobbing. Blossom held me tighter, and I sobbed and sobbed against her until her shirt was drenched with my tears.

"Oh, sweetie," she whispered, stroking my hair. "What did he do? What did he do to my sweet, little Annie?"

All pretenses were gone. I looked up at her in fear and whispered, "I tried so hard to make him stop. I screamed and screamed for you guys, but he'd taken me to a whole other wing of the manor where he knew you couldn't hear me. I tried to fight him off but he threw me and I hit the back of my head and he had by the throat and I... I couldn't make him stop! I couldn't make him stop!" I babbled and wailed. My body was convulsing in sobs. Blossom held me close. I couldn't get the words out about what he'd done, but she knew what I was saying.

"Oh, Annie, sweet Annie. I am so, so sorry. I didn't know he was capable of that," she whispered. "If I'd had any idea, if I'd had *any* idea... I'd never have let us go there. I should have kept you safe from him. I should have kept you safe."

I gave in fully to the tears, the convulsions of sorrow and anger, the fear, the pain, the betrayal. Blossom held me for a long, long time. When I finally had no more tears for the night, she tucked me into bed. She got me my big stuffed panda bear from the far side of the room. She even got me a glass of water. "You'll be a good mom someday, Blossom," I told her warmly. "Thank you for...." and I nodded, unable to put my gratitude into words.

"Any time of day or night, Annie, I am here for you."

I smiled, hugged my panda, and went to sleep.

April 29th

Before we left the house the next morning, I wrote out a check for my portion of the rent for the next few months. Globotek, via Edwin, was paying me a lot of money to be their superhero now. I was proud that I was no longer the weak link in the roommate financial chain. Neal looked at the check as if it might bounce, but he promised to cash it anyway.

We drove back to the compound and turned the transporter over to Edwin and a team of eager scientists. They started babbling to each other excitedly when they saw it. I was surprised to hear that all of them, including Edwin, were speaking in Chinese.

"We needed the best in the world," Edwin explained to me in English, "And even though the U.S. hates to admit it, the Chinese are *way* ahead of us when it comes to this type of spatial technology."

I gave the basic demonstration of how I'd been shown that it worked. What little I said was translated into

Chinese. Then the scientists jumped on their new toy like kittens on a ball of yarn. I headed down to the basement for another day of training with Chip and the Odds.

May 8th

The next couple weeks flew by. Chip, the Odds, and I practiced heat rays and freeze rays throughout every day. Most evenings after dinner, Rod and I would go for a walk. We didn't ever talk about serious things. We just enjoyed the fresh air. He liked to geek out on various topics – the way guys do – and tell me way more details than anyone ever needed to know about things like miniature war gaming figures (who knew they came in size 6 millimeter?) and European-style choose-your-own-adventure books (apparently, they're a thing). It was so hilariously random to listen to him. But it was a good feeling – making a new friend. I was growing fond of him.

Before we knew it, we were one day from go-time. I was late getting over to the cafeteria for lunch. When I arrived, I saw Edwin eating alone. I brought my tray over and joined him. As I sat down, I realized he wasn't technically *eating* alone. His bowl of soup was full to the brim. His salad was stacked in a neat little pyramid on its plate. His silverware sat clean on the tray.

"Not hungry?" I asked.

He looked up, startled, as if I had appeared out of nowhere.

"Oh, no," he said, "it's... no..." and he trailed off.

"Problems with something?" I sat down opposite him and began eating my chicken strips and fries. "Transporter not working?"

"Working perfectly," he replied blandly. "We sent someone up to the international space station just this morning and brought them back without a hitch."

"That's great news," I said.

"Hmmm..." he said. He pushed his knife, fork and spoon into neat parallel rows. "And tomorrow the ship will be close enough that we feel comfortable sending you all onto it," he said.

"How close is close enough?" I asked. I dunked my chicken strips into the honey mustard sauce and chowed down. I love chicken strips in honey mustard.

"About the same distance as Mars," he said.

I thought about it. "Doesn't the government know about the alien ship by now? Won't NASA or those SETI guys have seen it?"

Edwin nodded. "Oh, quite... certainly by tomorrow if they haven't already..."

This was getting nowhere. "So, what's getting you

down in the dumps, Edwin? It sounds like everything is just ducky."

Edwin stopped poking at his silverware and looked up at me. "Do you remember your first day at the mountain when Delphine scanned you and gave you that Compound to drink?"

I nodded.

"That was no ordinary painkiller you received," Edwin said, "and no ordinary scanner. It was Marguar technology that allowed us to scan your brain, and Marguar technology that gave us an exact mix of medicines to put your brain to rights. It wasn't a perfect cure, but it did in seconds what our planet's medicine would have taken months or even years to accomplish."

I remembered how instantly my stress had vanished after drinking that compound. But this was a more personal conversation than I was prepared for. "Where are you going with this?" I asked.

"Human technology is nowhere near the level of sophistication or advancement of the Marguars. We are decades if not centuries away from their capabilities. I am a man of science, Annie. The years I've been working in trade with the Marguars have been the most exciting of my life. The new technologies I have seen! The inventions and medicines the Marguars are trading with us — they are giving countless advances to humanity! It is truly miraculous — every bit of it. And we are one day away from losing it all."

I reflected on what he was saying. "You don't want to lose the trade with the aliens."

"Not at all!" he moaned. "Their technologies are like magic to us. How can we possibly let that go!"

"They are aliens who eat us and want to colonize and enslave our planet."

Edwin threw his fork down angrily, startling me. "That's all because of Jaliswack," he raged. "We'd had a good arrangement worked out with the Marguars. Trade negotiations were solid. But that Jaliswack.... *He* was the one who overstepped in his demands and began escalating tensions between us and them. If he had only let well enough alone, they never would have even tried to take over the mine, much less send an occupying force. Jaliswack is as honest as a dirty sock. The Marguars saw that. They *knew* they needed their own personnel involved, if they were ever going to get a fair deal out of him. And now it's all gone to hell, and we're going to start a war with our trade partners.... Oh, Annie, think of the technologies humanity will never see.... All because you and I destroyed our planet's first ever trade with this incredible race of creatures. It's all that damn Jaliswack's fault."

"Why didn't you stop Jaliswack before it got to this point?" I had to ask him.

Edwin sighed heavily. He pushed his glasses up his nose. "I'm not a brave man, Annie," he shrugged. "I'm not brave at all. Jaliswack is powerful and dangerous. You already know how he treated the workers in his mine. I've worked with him a long time and have seen many more stories of horror. If I opposed him, he could have me fired or even killed. He might threaten my folks or my children. And now, we're losing everything, because I did nothing sooner...."

I dipped my French fries into the honey mustard sauce and marveled at Edwin in silence.

"But you are brave, Edwin," I told him. "This entire resistance wouldn't exist without you. You and I are saving the world from some dangerous aliens who really will do us a lot of harm. No matter what the cost, think of the lives we are protecting and saving. You are a brave and honorable man, Edwin Peabody. I want to be like you when I grow up." I smiled.

He looked at me kindly. "Does that mean you've forgiven me for the way I forced the blood sample from you?"

I was surprised that he brought that up. I thought about it. "Yes, I have. The way those thugs grabbed me was scary. But I didn't know at the time about the Marguars and the planet being in danger. I think if I had been in your shoes, I would have felt just as desperate as you did."

Edwin nodded. "But I still did you wrong, Annie. So horribly wrong. Please know I will never do anything like that again."

I smiled at him. "Don't worry, Edwin. I know that now. You've treated me well while I've been here. I respect all that you're doing here, and I'm proud to be a part of it."

He smiled at me sheepishly and pushed his large glasses up his nose again. "Thank you, Annie. It means a good deal to me to hear you say that. And now if I may change the subject, I must tell you how fascinating this transporter is that you brought us. There are a few competing theories about how to transport matter at an atomic level, but the approach the creator of this one took is entirely..."

I listened and ate while Edwin launched into a stream of excited technobabble that I had absolutely no hope of understanding. But I enjoyed watching the nerd scientist in him resurfacing. He really was a hopeless nerd at heart. I liked him. I nodded excitedly and said, "Impressive!" at all the right moments. I had no idea what he was talking about, and I didn't pretend to try.

May 9th

It was go-time. We gathered in the laboratory where the transporter had been set up. The scientists were bustling about doing last minute checks on us, our gear, our bombs, and all other things technical. There was a buzz of excitement in the air as everyone prepared.

"Why don't we just transport a couple bombs up there and save time?" I whispered to Rod.

"In a ship this large, the placement of explosives is everything," Rod whispered back. "Besides, we want to copy their ship's hard drive. Just think about it. This species has actually managed to achieve interstellar travel. Imagine how much we could learn from getting our hands on some of that technology. It's too great an opportunity to pass up." With any luck, we'd download some more of the technologies that Edwin had been mourning the loss of yesterday.

Our team took our places in fighting formation in the

middle of the room, each of us standing on a small blue transport pad. We were clad for battle, armed with freeze rays and heat rays, and loaded up with all kinds of other gadgets. Clipped to our sleeve cuffs were transport coms, which would bring us back home when activated. In a pile between us, on their own transport pads, lay all the bombs and the detonator.

"Ready?" Chip asked us all.

I grinned. "Let's do it." Rod, Todd and Dodd gave up a cheer.

Chip nodded to the scientists. "Beam us up," he grinned.

The scientists at the transporter whispered a few final words to each other in Chinese. Then they grinned at us, engaged the controls, and the world evaporated around us.

We rematerialized someplace dark.

"Where are we?" I whispered after a moment. "Did we make it?"

A few flashlights popped on, and we took a look around. We were in a storage room of some kind. Large metal containers were lined up everywhere and stacked up high above our heads. Each container had Marguar symbols printed on it, presumably labeling the contents of each. Dodd was the most adept at reading the Marguar language. "Looks like it's mostly food storage compartments," he said, shining his flashlight from box to box. "And seeds. Boxes and boxes of seeds."

"Creeeeeepy!" Todd whispered.

We did a quick survey of our supplies and were pleased to see that everything was present and accounted for. Todd set to work. He pulled out two fancy electronic gizmos and began running a methodical sweep of the room with both, pointing them carefully in every direction.

"They're mapping the ship for us," he explained to me.

"Do they label where engineering is?" Dodd asked.

Todd rolled his eyes. "No. But they do track energy signatures, so we can tell which areas of the ship are generating lots of power."

"Sweet."

Todd finished the sweeps and handed one of the gizmos to Dodd.

"Okay," Chip took command. "Rod, Todd and I are going to fan out and set explosives throughout the ship. Dodd, you're going to hack into their mainframe and copy all you can. Right now, getting that information is as, if not more, important than getting this ship destroyed. Annie, your job is to protect Dodd. We'll meet back here at 1100 hours, set the charge, and activate our transport coms to get off this ship before it blows."

"Check," we all said. Rod and I gave an encouraging nod to each other. Then Chip, Rod and Todd picked up the bombs and headed out. Dodd and I huddled over the mapping gizmo and took a look.

"We need to get three levels down and about a

hundred yards that way," he said. "I think that's where we'll find their main communications array."

"Does that gizmo detect life signs, too?"

"Don't I wish!" Dodd said.

We poked our heads out of the door and peered down the dimly lit hallway. It looked like an armored tunnel. The walls were dark grey, metal and dirty. Black metal archways supported a domed ceiling. A few arched doors poked off on either side of the hallway. Anyone caught halfway down the hall would be a sitting duck.

We nodded silently to each other and headed out. We carried our heat rays at the ready, and Dodd checked his gizmo frequently, indicating with silent gestures when to turn down which hallway. As we walked, I made a mental map of the place. If anything happened to Dodd or the gizmo, I did not want to get lost in this place.

Suddenly, we turned a corner and not twenty feet down the hall from us stood a Marguar. The creature was gigantic. It must have towered over nine feet tall. We'd caught it by surprise. It roared when it saw us and puffed itself out like a blowfish – instantly ballooning up to twice its regular size. Its tentacled arms gesticulated wildly. Dodd and I gasped as we blasted it with our heat rays. The overgrown slug disappeared in a puff of rancid black smoke.

We looked at each other and grinned, breathing sighs of relief.

"That's good news," Dodd whispered. "We were over ten feet away from him. He didn't have his energy shield on."

"Good news, indeed," I whispered back. We continued silently through the halls of the ship and soon arrived at the communications center.

We peered inside. The room was large and round and dark. Black metal consoles dotted the walls. In the center of the room was a console with a mass of screens and keyboard interfaces. Two Marguars stood in front of it with their backs to us. All their eyes were focused on the different screens. The rest of the room was clear.

Two quick heat ray blasts later, we entered the room. Dodd set to work at the main console, surrounded by two plumes of quickly evaporating rancid smoke.

"How long is this going to take you?" I asked him.

"I haven't the slightest idea," he replied.

That's when the Marguars came pouring into the room.

"Copy that drive!" I yelled at him, "I'll cover you."

Dodd slipped underneath the console and began working. I stood in front and started firing like mad at the aliens. I blasted the heat ray at the three in front. Poof, poof, and poof, and they disappeared in wisps of smoke. There was a roar of belching and growls from the aliens behind them. One lurched over to a console on the wall and started hitting buttons with all four of his tentacled arms. I blew him into oblivion a second too late. Yellow lights started flashing everywhere and a loud siren sound burst out. The alarm. One more *Blammo!* and the last of the aliens vanished.

My heat ray beeped that it needed to recharge. I holstered it and switched to the freeze ray. I ducked my head under the console to check up on Dodd. Dodd had hooked up his alien gear to the network. The system was clicking away.

"Is it working?" I asked him.

"I sure hope so. If I'm right, it's copying the computer hard drive right now."

"How long will it take?"

Dodd laughed. "Do you really think I know that? I'm banking on the idea that aliens who can cross galaxies have created computers that copy data faster than ours do." I nodded.

More Marguars came slithering into the room. These

ones were armed with freeze rays. Firing madly with the level two trigger, I sent out shooting blue rays of icy smoke. The rays bounced harmlessly off their shields. "Dammit!" I yelled. "Shields up!" It was a warning for Dodd. Hopefully, these aliens didn't know he was there. They hit me with icy blast after icy blast, and they bellowed roars of surprise every time I failed to die.

But I wasn't causing any damage to them either. I had to get closer – inside their shields. I hopped onto the console and took a flying leap off the edge. I landed squarely in the center of the mass of blobby aliens. Just where I wanted to be. I fired off two quick shots and froze two of the five into solid icicle blobs. A tentacled arm slinked around me from behind. I grabbed my heat ray, dug it into the arm and shot it off. I whirled around and kept shooting. Puffs of rancid smoke appeared.

The remaining Marguars roared and hissed at me. One of them slurped around behind me. A tentacle wrapped around my waist and lifted me high up off the ground. A second and third tentacle wound around each of my wrists. The Marguar shook me violently back and forth in the air. He threw me against the far wall. I smacked into it and fell to the floor in a heap, dropping my weapons. The aliens fired their freeze rays at me again and again, belching and clearly growing frustrated that they were having no effect. I saw where my freeze ray had landed. There was a Marguar between me and it. I couldn't see the heat ray.

The Marguar started slurping toward me. Without my freeze ray to attack with, these blobs were a whole lot bigger than me and a whole lot stronger! They certainly could tear me limb from limb, and they were about to start trying.

I let loose a battle cry and charged directly at the Marguar that was between me and my freeze ray. My feet hit his blobby body, and I just kept running. His body bounced like putty as I ran up it. At the top of his head, I grabbed one of his eye stalks and punched him squarely in the eye. He screamed, and his eye began leaking out an inky black fluid.

More tentacles wrapped around my body. Two aliens had me – one by the feet and one by the arms. They began pulling at me. I screamed as they tugged at my limbs. They were going to literally rip me apart!

Blammo! Blammo! Blammo!

The three blobs vanished in puffs of rancid smoke. I fell through the air and landed hard on the floor. I looked up, and Dodd was standing there, heat ray in one hand and an alien hard drive in the other.

"Let's get out of here," he said. I breathed a sigh of relief. We grabbed my weapons and took off.

We ran quickly and quietly back through the ship and made it back to our starting room without discovering any more aliens. Chip was already there, hard at work on the detonator.

"Todd and Rod are finishing up setting the explosives." Chip said. "Once they're all primed, the detonator will register them, and we'll know it's safe to blow the ship."

"Where did you leave them?" I asked. "The Marguar know we're on board."

"Ha! Ya think?" said Chip, nodding at the blinking yellow lights and wailing siren. "Dodd, you got the hard drive?"

He nodded.

"Then take it and transport back home right now. Ain't

no reason to stall in getting you out of here."

Dodd nodded. "See you on the other side!" He stood up straight, hard drive in hand, and activated his transport com. In a second, he had disappeared.

Chip shook his head. "I sure hope that thing works the way it's supposed to."

Rod and Todd came rushing into the room. I breathed a sigh of relief when I saw Rod's face.

"We got a herd of blobs on our tail!" Todd was yelling. "Let's blow this place and get out of here."

Todd and Rod took defensive positions at the door while Chip fired up the detonator.

"Everything's synced. Thirty seconds till it blows."

I dashed over to join Rod and Todd. But as I ran, Rod screamed a scream that cut to the core of my being. A life-and-death scream. My body froze in horror, and for a second the world was traveling in slow motion. I watched Rod falling backwards into the room, screaming in agony. He was engulfed in a mass of flames. He had taken a direct hit from a heat ray. His clothing, his body, his skin were on fire.

Chip instantly fired a freeze ray at Rod, extinguishing the flames and coating him in a block of ice. "Get him out of here!" Chip yelled. I activated the transporter that was clipped to Rod's shirt sleeve.

"You'll be okay," I whispered to him through the ice. Rod's eyes met mine, and he disappeared.

"Fall back!" Chip was yelling.

Dodd and Chip stood protectively in front of the detonator. I stepped out in the hall to see what was coming our way. I gasped. In both directions, the hallways were crawling with Marguars. They were undulating everywhere: on the floors, the walls, even hanging from the ceiling. They were storming toward us. I looked back at Chip and Todd – defiant, but defenseless against these monsters. Rod's burning body was seared in my mind's eye. I couldn't let these guys suffer the same or worse.

"Sorry guys," I called out to them. I turned my freeze ray on them, pulled the level one trigger, and smoked both of them with a puff of the ray. The air cleared. They were both encased in small blocks of ice. Chip was mad at me. I could tell.

"I can't let you guys get hurt!" I yelled at him. I activated the transporters that were clipped on their wrists and sent them home to safety.

Ten seconds left on the detonator. I couldn't let the Marguars get to it and disarm it. Even as I thought this, they began pouring through the doorway. I fired my freeze ray and heat ray like mad. Pulse after pulse of heat ray and freeze ray hit me. I kept firing and kept taking them down. They pummeled me with shots. I was quickly overwhelmed. Tentacled arms reached around me and shook me. Out of the corner of my eye, I saw one tentacled creature lifting the detonator and eyeballing it curiously.

I could see the counter ticking down. 3, 2, 1, 0....

The white light of the explosion shot out. The tentacled arms gripping onto me evaporated. I shut my eyes and smiled. The world around me exploded.

It was dark.

Everything was quiet.

At first, I couldn't tell where I was or what was happening. Slowly, things came into focus. In every direction, charred remains of the spaceship were floating freely in the vacuum of space. I gasped in surprise. That's when I realized there was no air to breathe in. I looked down at my feet and saw that *I* was floating freely in the vacuum of space, too.

I laughed out loud – a silent, airless laugh. A piece of debris floated by me. I grabbed it and pushed off. I stretched out my arms like Superman, flying through the void. Then I motioned like I was swimming, which made absolutely no difference in my propulsion, but was a whole lot of fun. I flipped over and mimed the backstroke.

Then I got serious and surveyed the damage. There was nothing but carnage in all directions. The boys would be happy. We'd done a good job.

I looked down at my wrist. My transport com was still tucked safely under the edge of my super-suit. I reached for it, activated it, and sent myself back home.

A loud cheer went up as I rematerialized in the compound. A huge crowd was standing there. Chip, Dodd, Todd, Edwin. The Chinese scientists. The entire crew at the compound. "The ship's been blown!" I reported happily. More cheering.

"We know!" Edwin scolded me. "Five full minutes ago! We thought it had taken you with it."

"Meh," I shrugged cheerfully. "Explosions. Space vacuums. Takes more than that to take me down!" Then I sobered up. "Where's Rod? Is he okay?"

Edwin looked grim. "He's been severely burned, no doubt about it, and he's been rushed off to surgery. We're going to try some of the compounds from the latest trade shipment. The doctors will do all they can."

"Can I see him?"

Edwin shook his head. "I need you for something else right now. There's been a problem over at the mine. We need you to do one last thing."

Edwin and I rematerialized in a dark passageway.

"I can't see a thing," I complained. Edwin shushed me loudly. The beam of a flashlight blinked on.

"We're in one of the back corridors of the mine," he whispered. "The Marguars are guarding the entrance. We thought we'd have a better chance from behind."

"With all due respect," I whispered. "Why are you with me instead of Chip and the Odds?"

"These guys are hoping to negotiate, which means I *need* to talk with them. It means there's still a chance, Annie, to save relations between our species. But, be prepared. You are here in case I fail." I took that in and nodded silently.

"What are we up against?"

We crept through the mine as we whispered back and forth.

"The Marguars here on Earth found out about us invading their ship, and they'll certainly know by now that we've destroyed it. They've taken Jaliswack hostage and are threatening to kill him if their demands aren't met."

"Would that be so bad?" I asked.

Edwin rolled his eyes at me. "They'll also kill all the

miners."

Dammit. "What do they want?"

"I don't know yet," he whispered. "Stay here and wish me luck!"

"I got your back," I promised him.

The thin tunnel we'd been walking down opened up into a large cavern. I stayed back and hid behind a mine cart. Edwin stood up straight, rolled his shoulders back, pushed up his glasses, and marched out toward the aliens. I could hear a roar of disgruntled burps and squirts as the Marguars saw Edwin approaching. I peered around the corner to watch what was happening.

There were five Marguars in the main cavern of the mine. One of them stood (sat?) on top of a large rock. Two were guarding the elevator door. The last two were guarding a man whom I guessed was Oswald Jaliswack. He was tied to a pole. His portly stomach flopped over the ropes that held him bound. He was gagged. As Edwin approached, the guards raised their heat rays up to Jaliswack's head. I could see beads of sweat dripping down his face and nervousness in his eyes.

As Edwin marched forward, he donned a strange earpiece and raised the translating megaphone to his lips. "Put those guns down!" he ordered the Marguars. "You aliens are class-A fools if you think threatening that man does you any good. Jaliswack is the *only* damn human on this planet who sees any benefit in keeping you alive at all.

If you kill him, there's *no one* left to speak for you."

The lead Marguar ballooned up, roared, and belched.

"Yes, we did blow up your ship," Edwin shot back angrily at him. "And if you send another one, we'll blow up that one, too! You are our trade partners, and we're happy to have you as that. But you aren't allowed to invade us, set up a colony or attempt to take over our planet in any way, shape, or form!"

More roars from the Marguar.

"I don't care *what* Jaliswack promised you! Nor does anyone else on this planet. In fact, I daresay, after this whole affair is over with, he's not even going to be running this company. His leadership brought on a near-alien invasion. And while it was not a *bother* for us to clean up his mess and extinguish your pathetic, little invasion before it began, it has not left our investors very happy! Why, there are some people on the Globotek board who want every one of you squished like slugs. They don't even care about continuing trade with your people."

It dawned on me that Edwin was making this all up on the fly. I was impressed.

"Now, you folks are lucky you're talking to me," Edwin continued. He began to pace back and forth as he spoke. The eyestalks of all the Marguars rotated back and forth, following him.

"I *happen* to think you all are worthy trade partners. I *happen* to think that it's worth not just squishing you all where you stand. Our two planets have a good thing going in swapping our raw materials for your products, and I hope to help you continue this. Now, obviously, we can't let you run the mine anymore. You simply overstepped your bounds, and that means you've lost some privileges on this planet. But, we can still let you stay at the base, in your regular quarters higher up the mountain. You may come and go from this planet as you like, and *if* we stay happy with the products you provide, we should be able to keep things peaceful. Just between you and me, I frankly hope that you *can* keep up your side of the trade. If our investors started to doubt your usefulness to us, we might have to bring our ship over to your planet and take a closer look at what we might be able to make use of there."

The lead Marguar was silent. Its eyestalks shifted back and forth in the direction of the other Marguars. A few tentacles flapped in unusual patterns. The other Marguars began behaving in the same fashion. I guessed that I was seeing some type of Marguar sign language and they were debating how to respond to Edwin's threats.

A loud belch and a bellow emanated from the lead Marguar. I raised my freeze ray and braced to dash forward. But instead, the Marguar guards dropped their threatening poses and placed their heat rays on the ground. One of them sliced through the ropes that held Jaliswack, setting him free. The old man pulled the gag out of his mouth and walked over to Edwin's side, stretching and flexing as he did so. I breathed a huge sigh of relief.

Edwin nodded respectfully to the blobs. "Gentlemen, I thank you," he told them through his megaphone. "Your actions here are noted and celebrated as a turning point in our peoples' relations. We shall have to ask you to leave the mine now. You are free to return to your quarters upstairs. We shall invite you this evening for a celebratory dinner on the sky plaza. Then tomorrow morning, I shall send my new man over to draw up the details of our *new* trade arrangement."

The lead Marguar shuffled down toward Edwin and belched something to him in what sounded like a polite and respectful tone. Edwin tapped a small communicator that he was wearing on his wrist and spoke into it.

"The situation in the mine has been resolved. Our Marguar guests will be returning to their quarters now. See that they are treated with respect along their way.... Yes, that's an affirmative." Edwin turned back to the lead Marguar. "You are welcome and safe in this mountain. No one will hassle you here. I shall see you tonight at dinner on the sky plaza."

The Marguars burped toward him, shuffled into the elevator, and rode up away from the mine.

When they were gone, I dashed out of my hiding place. "Edwin, you were incredible!" I gave him a hug. "I didn't know you had it in you."

He blushed and pushed his glasses up. "Honestly, I didn't know I did either!"

Jaliswack nodded and smiled. "Peabody," he said, "Call me impressed. Fancy clever talk you came up with! Tricking them into thinking I'm not important and all that."

Edwin clapped his boss on the back. "I'm honored to hear you say that, sir. I like to think I've learned from the best, when it comes to trickery and deception." Then Edwin raised his communicator again and said, "He's coming your way now."

Familiar shimmering yellow lights appeared. In the split second before Jaliswack vanished, I saw the transport com that Edwin had placed onto the old man's back. Then Jaliswack was gone.

"Where did you send him?" I asked in awe.

"To a holding cell at our compound," Edwin replied. "He's going to stay there until the police are ready for him."

I stared at Edwin amazed.

He smiled. "As of right now, every single miner in this mountain is free to walk out of here. I daresay reports of their stories here will reach police ears rather quickly. And I daresay Jaliswack will have quite a bit to answer for. I just wanted to make sure that he'll be around to answer for it."

I gave Edwin another hug. "You're a good man, Edwin. A good, good man."

May 10th

Rod was lying on the hospital bed at the compound. His body was wrapped in so many bandages that he looked like a mummy. The bandages covered half of his face, but the eye that was visible was closed. He was sleeping. I sat perched on a stool at his bedside, watching him sleep. He looked so peaceful. I wondered what kinds of scars awaited him under those bandages. I was grateful he was alive.

Delphine, the nurse, came over to me and put her hand on my shoulder.

"Is he going to be okay?" I asked.

"He's had third degree burns to over forty percent of his body," she said, "We're using Compound 74690 from the Marguars, but even so, he's still got a long recovery ahead. Who knows how many more surgeries. The skin on his head was burned straight down to the skull. He's suffered extensive damage to his right arm. The surgeons are working on how much of it they can save and how much will have to be amputated. He's our first test case of this Compound, but we're hopeful that it will significantly reduce the amount of scarring. It's still too soon to tell."

I nodded, encouraged by her words, and Delphine quietly left the room. I still held the image of Rod from the ship in my head. Even with the near magical healing qualities of the Marguar Compounds.... his whole body had been on fire.... I reached my hand over to Rod and rested my fingers on his unburned hand.

"I'm sorry, Rod," I whispered to him. "I should have protected you. I let you down." I squeezed his hand lightly.

Rod opened his eyes and looked up at me. His mouth was covered with bandages, but his visible eye seemed to twinkle a happy spark. He squeezed my hand back. Then he closed his eyes. Within seconds, he was asleep again.

I sat there holding his hand a long time. While I sat with him, I reflected on all that had happened to me in the past month and a half. Everything I had been through and everything I had seen and done... from the first day at Globotek until this moment here, holding the hand of a dear, new friend.

I realized I had one thing left to do.

I sent a quick text to Blossom and told her I needed her. Then I stood up, gently kissed Rod on the forehead, and marched off to the armory.

For one last time, I holstered my freeze ray. I made my

way to the room where they kept the transporter. No one was there, which was good. I couldn't let anyone get in my way on this one. I found the transporter and looked it over.

The Chinese scientists hadn't built a new transporter or even much modified the original. They had simply added a more powerful interface to the device. They had created the transport pads and coms to allow for easy identification of the matter to be transported. They had installed a monitor with mapped coordinates of the entire planet, on up into space, and out almost as far as Venus, so that it was equally easy to identify where to send something to. I played with the interface until I got a text back from Blossom. Glancing around to make sure no one was watching, I threw a blanket over the transporter, hefted it up, carried it out the front door of the compound, and carefully set it down in the trunk of Blossom's waiting SUV.

As we sped away from the compound, I laughed out loud. "That was sure easier than I thought it would be!"

"You're the woman who saved the world, Annie," Blossom grinned. "You're supposed to do the impossible."

"Ha!" I said wryly, "Yeah... Superhero Annie gets away with blatant thievery!"

"We're going to return it," Blossom reminded me.

"True, true, true..." I replied. "We only need it for tonight."

*　　*　　*

126

It was well into the evening by the time we arrived at Lord Feathering's manor. Blossom had made good with her uncle, claiming that the men from Globotek had been threatening us both, blackmailing us to get access to the manor. So when her SUV drove up to the wrought-iron gate, it opened right up for her. She parked by the three-headed dragon fountain and took my hand.

"Do you want me to come in with you?" she asked.

"Naw, I'll go first." I shook my head confidently. "I got to do this by myself."

"You gonna be okay?" she asked.

I grinned and shrugged. "Up, up, and away!" I joked.

Freeze ray holstered at my side and hidden under my long red sweater, I strode up to the door.

Lord Feathering answered the door. "Miss Annie!" he smiled when he saw it was me. "You came here with Blossom? I am so delighted to see you. Come in, come in, come in. Would you like some tea?"

"You may pour me tea," I told him evenly. "I'm here to speak to you about something."

"Absolutely, my darling Annie," he replied. "Let us sit and have a cup." I followed him into his creepy living room while he kept talking. "I am so grateful to see you've escaped those Globotek hooligans who were holding you captive. I'm so very glad you made it safely back to me. Fear not, my darling Annie. I will keep you safe from here on out."

I sat down on the red velvet sofa and let him pour me tea. I was astonished by what he was saying. This idiot really seemed to think I was returning to him. I'd never seen anyone so delusional. I couldn't believe I had once admired and respected this man. I couldn't believe I had once blushed at the glow of his smile. But that was a lifetime ago.

This man turned out to be evil inside. He had terrified me, strangled me, beaten me, and worse. For days, I hadn't been able to close my eyes without seeing images of what he had done to me. I hadn't been able to breathe without remembering the smell of his body against mine. Sleeping and waking had both been a nightmare. But now all that, too, was a lifetime ago.

I was Annie Glenn. I had fought aliens in hand-to-hand combat. I had disintegrated them and frozen them solid. I had run up the body of an alien and punched it in the eye. I had used my body to shelter my teammates, to save their lives and get them safely back to Earth. I had free-floated in the abyss of space and lived to tell the tale.

I was a superhero now. This man in front of me was nothing. He was small, delusional, and pathetic.

I sipped my tea.

The disgusting fellow sat in the chair opposite me, leaning over toward me and babbling away about how I would live safely and happily with him from here on out.

"Lord Feathering," I interrupted him. "I am not returning to you. I am not even here to listen to you talk. I am here to tell you something."

"Oh?" he asked. His blue eyes shone at me with curiosity and anticipation.

"When I first met you, I respected you. I thought you were special – that you could save me – that you would take care of me." I stood as I spoke and looked down at him in the chair. "But you didn't save me. And you didn't take care of me. You betrayed my trust. You threatened me. You beat me. You choked me. You raped me."

Saying the word out loud shook me for a second.

Lord Feathering stood up abruptly and pulled himself to his full height. "Now, wait a second, Miss Annie! I did absolutely nothing of the sort!" he yelled. "How dare you accuse me of such a thing! What's wrong with you? What's making you say such things?"

He stepped close to me and used his full height to tower down over me. His eyes flashed in anger. But I'd faced down Marguars four times his size. He had no power over me anymore.

"You planned the entire thing from the moment we left the lab," I shot back at him. "You intentionally took me to an isolated area of the manor, where you *knew* no one would be able to hear or help me. You isolated me and forced yourself on me. I tried to push you away. I screamed for you to stop. But you beat me and punched me and strangled me and raped me. You're a pathetic man, Lord Feathering. Pathetic and delusional and evil and cruel. You should be in jail for the rest of your miserable life."

He was quiet. I thought for a split second that he would admit it. I thought he was about to apologize to me for what he'd done. But then he broke into that same sickening smile I'd seen the night he raped me.

"Is that your plan, then, little girl?" he hissed. "Are you going to report me to the authorities and try to get me found guilty? No one will ever believe your fairy tales. It will be easy for me to see to that. No, no, no, Annie, what's going to happen now is that you are going to come back to me. You are going to stay here, and you will be mine. I will see to it that you have no other option."

I shrugged. "I have no desire to deal with you anymore. You do deserve to be in jail, but I don't want to deal with you enough to send you there. Luckily," I added, "I have other options."

I pulled out my freeze ray and blasted him at point blank range. When the mist cleared, he was encased in a block of ice from his nose down. I grinned briefly at my aim. He wouldn't waste the air by talking anymore, but his ears were free to hear all I wanted to tell him.

I looked up to see that Blossom had come in with the transporter. "Perfect timing!" I smiled at her. We set the transporter in front of the ice block.

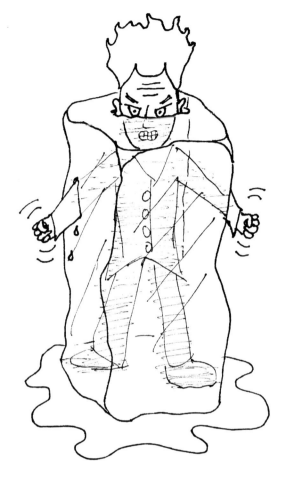

"Some lovely Chinese scientists did a little tweaking to your transporter. It's amazing how well it works now!" I told him brightly.

I tossed one of the transport pads on the ground. Blossom and I slid him in his block of ice squarely onto the pad. I fired up the transporter and found my desired destination.

"Goodbye, Archie Feathering," I called out to him. "I hope you rot in hell."

I engaged the transporter and watched as he shimmered in a yellow glow and vanished.

When he was gone, I looked up to see Mrs. Westcott standing in the doorway to the kitchen. I briefly wondered how long she'd been standing there. But she never told me, and I never did ask. She just walked over to me and clapped me on the back. "Well done, Annie Glenn," she said. "Well done."

"Where did you send him?" Blossom asked me.

"A tiny deserted island in the middle of an ocean," I replied. "It's monsoon season there right now."

Blossom grinned and tackled me in a bear hug. I started laughing and crying both at the same time. I gave my friend a big hug back.

A Few Months Later....

Well, dear diary, it's been a while, so I ought to catch you up on all that's happened. The cover-up stories kept news of alien life out of the mainstream media. But those in the know are preparing for a possible second wave.

The Feds arrested Jaliswack for a laundry list of crimes. The miners are all starting to get their days in court, along with hoards of other people whom Jaliswack screwed over throughout the years. He's currently awaiting trial and is likely to spend the rest of his days in prison.

Meanwhile, Blossom pulled some strings in her family and got the keys to be the new caretaker of the manor. No one in the family has heard anything from *him* since he disappeared. We're all hoping he never returns. Blossom and Neal have moved into the manor. Blossom is hard at work de-creepifying the place. Neal is in computer-geek heaven.

Blossom has also opened up the manor as temporary

free housing to the men who were enslaved in Jaliswack's mines. The place is crawling with social workers who are helping all those people put their lives back together and reconnect with their families. Blossom is taking charge of the whole operation and is setting up a non-profit organization solely devoted to the cause, so that she can continue to fight human trafficking even after she's helped all the former miners. Looks like she's found her new career path – talk about saving the world!

Edwin has managed to stay out of jail, and I'm oh-so-happy about that. He is now overseeing the trade relations with the Marguars. But he's also hedging his bets. On the one hand, he's receiving, processing, and selling miraculous new inventions and miracle medicines from the Marguars. On the other hand, he has finished rebuilding Laboratory 735 and is quietly creating a whole army of super-soldiers just like me. He wants to be ready in case the Marguars decide to invade again. From what I hear, the first ones to sign up for it were Chip, Dodd, and Todd. (Good for them!)

Rod is still in the hospital, but he is doing well considering. He looks like half of his face is melted off. His right ear is gone. He ended up losing his hand from the mid-forearm down. He has massive scarring and more surgeries to come. But his hospital room has a constant stream of brothers, cousins, aunts, uncles, and parents coming to stay with him and help him. Three of his brothers are in town right now. I visit Rod once a week at least, and I am always there when he has a surgery. Once he's up and about again, he's going to take that backpacking trip across Australia that he's dreamed about for so long. Every day is a struggle, but he's keeping his spirits up.

Edwin offered me a job – pretty much anything I wanted, really – but I turned him down. I told him I'd be on standby, though, if there ever is a second invasion. If the world needs saving again, he can count on me. He had Globotek cut me a gigantic check as thanks for saving the world and all. Globotek said I deserved it, and I rather agreed with them. I bought myself a new car – a sexy, little, black convertible. And I bought a one-bedroom condo by a lake, not too far from Blossom's manor. The condo has a large window and balcony that overlooks the lake, and there's a lovely sunset view every evening on the water. It's a little piece of heaven.

I had a housewarming party and invited Chip and the Odds and Blossom and Neal. While we were eating pizza and talking late into the night, Todd surprised the heck out of me by asking me out on a date. He looked so hopeful and cute, and I was so touched that he'd asked. I turned him down as gently as I possibly could. My life has been so crazy lately. I need it to be boring and uneventful for a while.

Besides, I got other things to think about. Thanks to my saving-the-world thank-you check, I finally have enough money to pay for beauty school. I've signed up for classes and start on Monday. I can't wait. My dream of cutting and styling women's hair will be a reality before I know it. I feel overwhelmed and lucky. A whole new chapter in my life is beginning.

I think I'm going to get a cat.

THE END

ABOUT THE AUTHOR

Rosemary Sixbey lives with her fabulous son, beloved husband and endearing cats in a town that she loves called Renton, Washington. She is older than she looks, and, as far as she is aware, she has never saved the world.